Dragon's Egg

by Sarah L. Thomson

Greenwillow Books

An Imprint of HarperCollins *Publishers*

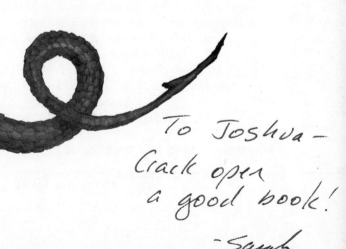

To Joshua —
Crack open
a good book!

—Sarah

Dragon's Egg
Copyright © 2007 by Sarah L. Thomson
All rights reserved. No part of this book may be used or reproduced in any manner whatsoever without written permission except in the case of brief quotations embodied in critical articles and reviews. Printed in the United States of America. For information address HarperCollins Children's Books, a division of HarperCollins Publishers, 10 East 53rd Street, New York, NY 10022.
www.harpercollinschildrens.com

The text type is Cochin.

Library of Congress Cataloging-in-Publication Data
Thomson, Sarah L.
Dragon's egg / by Sarah L. Thomson.
p. cm.
"Greenwillow Books."
Summary: Mella, a young girl trained as a dragon keeper, learns that the legends of old are true when she is entrusted with carrying a dragon's egg to the fabled Hatching Grounds, a dangerous journey on which she is assisted by a knight's squire.
ISBN 978-0-06-128848-7 (trade bdg.)
ISBN 978-0-06-128847-0 (lib. bdg.)
[1. Dragons—Fiction. 2. Eggs—Fiction. 3. Voyages and travels—Fiction. 4. Knights and knighthood—Fiction. 5. Fantasy.] I. Title.
PZ7.T378Dqt 2007 [Fic]—dc22 2007009145

First Edition   11 12 13 LP/RRDB 20 19 18 17

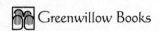 Greenwillow Books

To Julian—thanks for the idea
and to R.D.—just thanks
—S.L.T.

Chapter One

"Mella! Hurry and fetch the eggs!"

"I'm just going, Mama!" Mella stepped out onto the back porch of the Inn. Despite her mother's words, she didn't hurry, pausing to tie a scraggly red ribbon around the end of her thick blond braid. The sunlight was just brushing the tops of the dark spruce trees, and above them, softened by a faint blue mist, Mella could see the peaks of the Dragontooth Mountains.

She picked up a pair of heavy gloves and a basket lined with soft, damp moss and went to gather the eggs.

On a normal day, Redtail would be peering over the gate, waiting to have her spine scratched.

Mella kept a long stick leaning against a fence post for that purpose. But today Redtail was off in a far corner of the pen, and although Zip and Zap edged over to get their ears rubbed, neither seemed as eager for the attention as they usually did. In fact, Zap pulled his head out from under Mella's hand to sniff at the air, his nostrils wide and his stubby wings quivering.

Mella glanced over her shoulder, wondering what he could have seen or smelled, but she saw nothing except the Inn, the stable, and the yard. Everything as simple and ordinary as good plain bread. Perhaps they were in for a storm, though she could not spot a cloud in the sky. Changes in the weather sometimes made the herd nervous.

Mella shrugged and unlatched the gate. Digger stopped poking his long, thin snout into the sparse grass of the pen long enough to look up and snort a greeting. Nothing ever disturbed Digger in his single-minded pursuit of anything edible.

"And hello to you, too, old boy." Mella slipped into the pen and shut the gate behind her. "Now,

Angel . . . now, Snow . . ." She patted the warm, scaly bodies jostling about her knees. "Best not to keep Mama waiting for those eggs."

Each of the brooding dragons sat atop a heap of stone and gravel the creature had scooped up with claws and snout. A dragon could, at will, alter the natural color of its scales to blend in with its surroundings. Most of the females with eggs had already done so, changing from warm brown or gray green or dusty black to a mottled mud color. It took more than a quick look to distinguish a dragon from her nest.

Mella crooned to her herd and rubbed their ears as she slipped her gloved hand underneath them to find the eggs, the heat of their scaly bodies bringing a red glow to her cheeks. On most mornings the dragons would be glad to see her, a happiness that always soaked into her like sunlight. But today half the beasts seemed infected with the same restlessness that had taken Redtail and Zap. Blackie even hissed at Mella and raised the crest along her neck in warning as the girl came to kneel by her nest.

"Blackie!" Astonished, Mella sat back on her heels to stare. "What's come over you this morning?" The little dragon with the dark scales looked properly ashamed of herself and nuzzled at Mella's elbow in apology. "I should hope so," Mella scolded gently as she retrieved two eggs. She had a dozen in her basket now, cushioned by damp moss to keep them safe. Some were soft brown flecked with gold, some the grayish green of river stones, some white as fresh cream. All steamed slightly in the cool air as if they'd just come from an oven.

"Mella! Where are you with those eggs?"

Mella's mother had stepped out onto the porch to call her. Leaving Blackie with a quick scratch under her jaw, Mella slipped her hand beneath Vixen's body, hoping for one more egg. The Inn was full of hungry guests to feed. There! Tucking the last egg into the moss, Mella set off at a run across the yard, careful not to jostle her basket or crack its contents.

"What a smell of dragons!" Mella's sister, Lilla,

slicing bread at the table, wrinkled her nose as Mella hurried into the kitchen.

"Mind your manners and count your blessings," Mama said crisply. "If Mella didn't have the touch with the dragons, we'd have to hire a keeper for them, and there'd be no more money for your pretty ribbons, my girl." When their mother turned back to the fire, Lilla tossed her head so the green ribbons that matched her eyes and the trim on her second-best dress danced in the air.

Mella stuck her tongue out at Lilla. She liked the tindery, sulfury smell of dragons, no matter what her sister said. Lilla was sixteen and hard to please.

"A dozen, well done." Using only one hand, Mama deftly cracked the eggs into her big blue mixing bowl. "You do have the touch with the dragons, sweet, just like your Gran."

Mella twisted away a little as if she hadn't noticed Mama's hand reaching out to stroke her hair.

"Fetch me some butter from the cold room, love." Mama began to beat the eggs briskly. "Lilla, mind how you slice that loaf!"

After dropping her basket by the door and tucking her gloves in her pocket, Mella ran down the stone stairs to the cold room. Built deep into the hill behind the Inn, its rock walls trapped a damp chill even in the height of summer. Mella, a crock of butter in her hands, had to stop and stand still a moment, squeezing her eyes shut to fight the stinging behind them.

Foolish. It had been nearly a year now since Gran died. And Gran had never had the least patience with crying. "Tears mend nothing," she'd say. "Work mends all."

Nearly a year since Gran died. And then there had been Lady.

Mella rubbed her hand hard over her eyes. Certainly there was enough work at the Inn to mend anything, especially at breakfast time. She ran back up the stairs to the kitchen, the heels of her shoes clattering.

"Like a herd of cows!" Lilla said, disgusted, slapping trays of sliced bread down on the table. "Just because those overgrown lizards like you, don't think you needn't do your share here. How long can it take to fetch some butter?"

Mella made a face. "It's not *my* fault Jonas Evadson kissed Betheline behind the smithy yesterday. You needn't yell at *me*!"

"Jonas Evadson, is it?" Mama looked up from giving a final stir to a batch of porridge in an iron pot over the hearth.

"Oh!" Lilla dropped the bread knife and snatched at Mella's braid. Mella darted to the far side of the table, out of range. Then their father came in with an armful of firewood and asked why breakfast was taking so long when the guests were getting hungry waiting.

Porridge steaming in blue-glazed bowls, topped with golden honey and fresh white cream. Slices of brown bread warm from the oven. Thick strips of salty bacon. And, of course, eggs. Everyone knew that the Inn served dragon's eggs for breakfast, as only Mella's mother could make them: beaten soft and fluffy, light as clouds, with that *tang*, that wildness to the flavor that made people come from Dragonsford and even farther away just for a taste.

Mama stood by the fire, watching with a hawk's eye as the eggs hissed and sizzled in the huge iron skillet. Mella filled trays and poured tankards of mild brown ale. Lilla flounced through the door, her ribbons fluttering, to serve.

"The stranger wants more ale," she said, a little breathless, leaning into the doorway and thrusting an empty pitcher at Mella.

The stranger! Mella had almost forgotten the man who'd arrived after dark last night. After handing the full pitcher back to Lilla, she stuck her head through the door to the Inn's common room to get a proper look.

Most of the guests at the Inn were farmers and merchants on their way to or from the market at Dragonsford, well known to Mella's family, their faces as familiar as the geese returning in the spring. It was rare that a true stranger passed by. But the man at the table near the hearth was such a one. He'd traveled far and had two horses, a pack mule, and enough baggage to cross the king-dom, along with a boy to look after it.

He was eating quietly, looking at no one. Younger than Mella's father, he had skin as dark as the traders from the far south who came for the summer fair at Dragonsford. His linen shirt was unembroidered, and his curly black hair was trimmed close to his skull. Everything about him, Mella thought, seemed neat and plain and perfectly simple. But that did little to explain why the common room was quieter than usual, or why so many sidelong glances were being cast his way. Or why Lilla had put on her second-best gown and her new ribbons for serving today.

"My best bargain," Atwin of Addsley was saying to Mella's father. He pulled a golden chain out from under his shirt to show a long, curved, bone white ornament dangling from it. "Genuine dragon's tooth. A fact. And not your little farm dragons either. The true ones, old ones, bigger than a house, fire-breathers."

A dragon's tooth! Mella edged forward into the

room, letting the door swing shut behind her, as Atwin gazed at his treasure. "And he sold me a dozen, the fool! Hardly knew what he had. This will make my fortune."

"A fraud."

The stranger's voice was low but keen. Heads turned. Talk died down.

"What do you say?" Atwin drew himself up.

"I said you were deceived." The stranger didn't stir in his seat, only lifted his eyes to meet Atwin's. "A bear's tooth, most likely. Or the great hunting cat's. Not a dragon's."

"Aye, I'm afraid he's right, Atwin," Mella's father said with a grimace of sympathy. "You'll not make your fortune on this trade."

Atwin pulled the chain over his head to stare at the shard of white ivory in dismay. "But . . . it cannot . . . I gave the man twenty gold, and two lumps of Tyrene amber besides!" Suddenly he grinned wide enough to show the gaps where back teeth were missing. "Well, if I did not know, neither will my customers!" He laughed loudly, and

Mella saw her father relax a little. Disputes in the common room were bad for business.

"Indeed, Atwin, you should have known better," Da said, chuckling as he refilled the merchant's tankard with ale. "Dragon's teeth! You might as well buy fairy's wings or mermaid's scales."

"But there used to be," Mella protested. She wished she could have gotten a better look at the pendant before Atwin tucked it away in a purse at his belt. "True dragons. In the old days."

Da laughed and tugged her braid. "Aye, in the old days. Along with giants and trolls and goblins. You've listened to too many of your grandmother's stories, sweet."

Mella blushed and scowled, tossing her head to twitch her braid free. Why should he treat her like a toddling baby? "There *were*," she insisted. "King Coel drove them into the mountains." Everybody knew that. It was history, not story. Coel had fought dragons to save the kingdom, and not farm dragons like Zip or Zap. But true dragons, huge and ferocious and magical . . .

"That was a thousand years back," Da argued mildly. "Oh, it makes a grand story. And if I were king, I'd be sure it was written down in every history book. But tales grow in the telling. I'd not be surprised if Coel did no more than clear out those little common dragons from the woods so farmers could clear the land and sow their crops. Who knows the truth of it now?"

"Some do."

It was the stranger again. And this time the room didn't just grow quieter. It hushed completely. Everyone turned and stared.

The attention didn't seem to trouble the man at all. "There have been true dragons in these mountains for years beyond counting," he said, lifting his head slowly to look over the company with an impassive face and steady eyes. "Since Coel's great victory, it has been the efforts of my order that has kept the beasts away from human farms and fields."

"Your order, master? And what might that be, pray?" Mella could tell that Da didn't care for the direction the conversation was taking. Not that the stranger was angry or rude. On the contrary, his voice and manner were perfectly courteous. It was something about how calm he was, Mella thought. And how certain he seemed of what he was saying. And yet, what he was saying was . . .

"I am Damien Damerson," the man said, bending forward slightly in what seemed a courtly little bow, even from his seat on a low stool. A pendant around his neck, what looked like a narrow arc of white ivory on a golden chain, swung loose, and he tucked it back inside his shirt. "Knight of the Order of Defenders."

"Defenders?" Da asked skeptically. "Defenders against what?"

Damien lifted one eyebrow. "Against dragons, of course."

Chapter Two

Mella waited for the common room to break out in laughter. But no one so much as chuckled. No one stirred, either.

"There have been signs," Damien said. His quiet voice reached into every corner. Mella saw Lilla standing with her pitcher poised over a cup. Mama leaned in the doorway to the kitchen, her mouth slightly open.

"Some in my order can read the stars," Damien continued. "Reports have reached us. A farmer at Applegate lost two cows, and their bones were never found. In Grimsby, a hunter saw a winged shadow against the moon, and when he shot at it, it cried out in a voice like no man has ever heard."

"Wolves." Da looked uneasy. Applegate was not far away, and Grimsby even closer. "It was a hard winter. The packs are hungry."

"Hungry enough to eat a cow, bones and all?" Damien shook his head. "The signs have led me here."

"The only dragons you'll find at the Inn are in my farmyard," Da said firmly. "More ale, master? My wife will be happy to stir up another batch of dragon's eggs. Much the tastiest way to encounter them, I assure you. Atwin, another plate?"

"No, I thank you," Atwin answered with a doubtful glance at Damien. "I believe I'll be on my way this morning. The market won't wait, you know."

"Mella, get back to the kitchen," Da ordered, frowning.

Mella groaned when she saw the stack of dishes on the kitchen table. They would scarcely be finished before it would be time to start the midday meal. And it was Lilla's turn to wash, but she was lingering in the common room so she could keep an eye on the stranger. The knight. The dragon-slayer.

"The madman," Da said, coming through the door with a scowl on his face. "Driving my customers away with his talk. The half-wits are taking him seriously."

"Oh, don't fret." Mella's mother was tossing leftovers into a slop bucket for the dragons. "He'll be on his way soon enough, and the common room will be full for two weeks after to talk him over."

"He's a fool."

"So he pays in good coin, he may be whatever he pleases. Girls, get a start on those dishes."

Lilla came back into the kitchen reluctantly. She scrubbed, and Mella dried. When the last plate and tankard were clean, Mama appeared, as if by magic, behind them.

"Lilla, go and wipe the tables in the common room. Mella, I've an errand I need you to run." Mama held out a basket with two apples, a wedge of fresh white cheese, and a dragon's egg left over from the morning, all nestled in a clean white napkin. "I need more willow bark and red clover and some hawthorn berries. Mind you be polite to old Cate."

Mama didn't have to tell her. Mella was always civil to Cate, who might be a witch and might not be, but who certainly knew the use of every root, berry, and flower that grew in the forests and on the mountainside. This time, Mella was not quick enough to dodge Mama's hand as it came down to smooth her hair.

"You do very well with the dragons, sweet," Mama said, her voice gentle. "Your Gran would be proud."

Mella snatched up the basket and ran out of the kitchen on her errand. But halfway across the yard she paused, noticing someone by the dragon pen. Who was it? A boy her own height. But the stable boys knew better than to bother the dragons. Snow was hissing, and Zap had his head through the fence rails, his ears flat against his neck, his crest up and bristling—a sign he'd bite soon if whoever was too near did not back away. As restless as the herd had been that morning, it would not take much to set them all in a dither now. And there would go the eggs for tomorrow.

Mella may have been no more than twelve, and a keeper for barely a year, but she knew better than to let someone bother her dragons. She headed over.

"Leave them be! You'll upset them."

The boy jumped a little and looked guilty. "I only wanted a look."

"Well, don't." Mella planted herself firmly in front of the gate, blocking his way. "They don't like people."

Zap reared up so that his head was over the fence and puffed out a cloud of steam from his nostrils. The boy stepped back, a shock of fair hair tumbling over a pleasant, mild face.

"You see?" Mella turned to push Zap down and scratched behind his ears to soothe him. The boy retreated several steps, and the dragons settled down.

"You said they don't like people," he remarked as Mella checked the latch on the gate. "But they don't mind you."

"Of course not. I have the touch. I'm a keeper."

An odd mixture of pride and uneasiness stirred inside Mella as she said it. Well, didn't she have something to be proud of? Keepers were rare, and it didn't always run in families. And hadn't Mama just said that she did well with the dragons?

But then, Mama wasn't a keeper herself. Despite all her years at the Inn, she didn't know much about dragons. It was Gran who had known.

Mella gave the gate a smack with her hand to be sure the latch would hold and turned to take a closer look at the boy. He was a stranger to her, and it took her a moment to place him. Of course! He must be the knight's servant boy.

"Is your master really a dragon-slayer?"

"Oh, has he done the speech already?" The boy's face grew mock solemn. "'There are signs. The signs have led me here.' He does it at every inn."

Mella's heart sank, heavy as stone. She hardly knew why she felt such dismay. What did it matter if Damien were a charlatan or a cheat? He was hardly the first of those to stay at the Inn.

"Why does he do it?" she asked. If Damien's speech were nothing but a conjuror's trick, what was the secret behind it? What did the man hope to gain?

"Now he'll hear all the news, that's all. Everyone who's lost a cow or a sheep, or who's heard something in the underbrush at night, will come and tell him. So if there's a dragon about, by nightfall he'll know where to look."

"So there might be? A dragon?" It was not as though she *wanted* a huge, fire-breathing, cow-eating beast in the woods nearby. Still, Mella felt her heart lift.

"*He* thinks there might be. But I've been his squire two years now, and I've not seen so much as a scale."

"But he's truly a knight?"

"Oh, aye. The Defenders. It's a very old order. But there are only a few left now." The boy looked at her curiously, as if wondering why she was so interested. "I suppose, if I'd spent my whole life training to fight dragons, I might see one behind every bush too."

"But you don't think there are any."

The boy looked squarely at her with clear gray eyes and shrugged. "I think the hunter at Grimsby saw an owl against the moon, and the farmer at Applegate lost his cows to wolves. Since you ask me. And I'm Roger. Though you didn't ask me that. And you?"

Mella turned on her heel and walked out of the yard.

She was halfway to Cate's before she started to regret her rudeness. After all, the boy was only answering her questions. But how could he be so sure that Damien was wrong, that dragons no longer existed? He was as bad as her father, thinking there was nothing in the world beyond the Inn and the next harvest.

Even when Gran, Da's own mother, would say that the mountains held strange things, old things, he never paid her any mind. "Time goes differently around rock and stone," Gran would say. "The mountains think their own thoughts, and they don't pay much heed to such short-lived things as us." But her son would have none of it.

And this boy, Roger, he was another of the same kind. Angry all over again, Mella turned aside from the main road and made her way up the narrow track that was a shortcut to Cate's cottage. Through the gap in the hawthorn hedge; up the bank, thick with wild violets; over the stepping-stones that lay across the shallow stream. Normally it was a walk Mella enjoyed. And that was another thing to put to Roger's account: making her cross enough to spoil what should have been a pleasant stroll in the woods on a summer's morning.

What was that smell?

Mella wrinkled her nose. Something dry and smoky. Burnt, like charcoal. Had someone been cutting trees and making charcoal up here? It seemed a strange place to choose.

Off to Mella's right, the little stream danced clear and cold over rocks as it spilled out of a cave in the hillside. When Mella was younger and Lilla would still play with her, they'd explored that cave, pretending to find treasure, jewels and old coins, a bandit's stash or a pirate's hoard.

A trickle of gray smoke eased out from the cave's mouth. Was someone there? A traveler? But this place was half an hour's easy walk from the Inn. Any honest traveler would have hurried on to shelter, even with night falling.

What about travelers who were less than honest? Smugglers? Outlaws?

The wise thing to do would be to run straight home and tell Da.

Mella found she was standing right outside the cave, on the edge of the stream, holding her breath and listening.

She could not hear a sound. Later, she would think that should have warned her. On a bright summer day, the trees should have been full of birds, twittering and squawking and chirping, and squirrels chattering and rustling in the leaves. But she could hear nothing beyond the breeze and the water splashing over stones at her feet.

Just one quick look. It might be nothing. She'd feel a fool if she told Da there were bandits in the cave, only to find that some of the village children had kindled a fire and forgotten to stamp it out. And she'd felt like a fool once already this morning, in the common room at breakfast.

Mella crouched down so she would not be outlined against the light and peeked into the cave.

There *was* a fire, a circle of dim, red coals. No bandits, though. Just the rough, muddy floor, the ceiling lost in the gloom, and the little stream, spilling out of a crack in a stone wall to run dark and quick through the cave and out into the sunshine.

Thank goodness she had not gone running to Da with stories of outlaws. He would have teased her for months. Still, that fire should not be left burning, even on bare rock. Mella went to put it out.

Why did it smell so strongly of sulfur in here? The rotten-egg reek was worse than the dragon pen when it needed cleaning.

Mella scuffed the coals aside with her shoe, scattering them. And paused.

Something that was not a charred piece of wood glowed black in the heart of the fire. Heat rising off it made the air waver. Mella blinked.

It was round and smooth as an egg. In fact, that's what it looked like. An egg in a nest of fire.

A good thing she still had her gloves in her pocket. They were dragonhide, soft and supple but strong enough to protect her hands from any kind of heat. Every keeper had a pair. These had once been Gran's. Mella slipped them on and reached into the fire to pick the thing up.

It was black and glossy, large enough that she had to cradle it in two hands, and so hot she could feel it even through the dragonhide. Was it just a rock worn smooth by the water in the stream? It must be. But even so, it was beautiful. Fascinated, Mella watched as colors seemed to shift and swim beneath the dark surface—pine green, molten red, the deep blue of a sky on a clear day when the last light is fading.

She'd found a treasure in the cave after all.

Chapter Three

Mella knew she must keep her discovery safe. Who had put it in the fire? Would they come back for it? At the thought, her fingers tightened around the object she held. Maybe she should have felt guilty for snatching the thing away, for taking it with her. Was it odd that she didn't? But she couldn't stop to think about it, couldn't wonder now. This . . . rock, gem, whatever it was—it was hers now. She needed to take care of it.

Moving quickly now, Mella hurried out of the cave. The cheese, apples, and egg for Cate she wrapped in the linen napkin and tucked safely into a niche between two clean, water-washed rocks.

She picked moss, dampened it in the stream, and used it to line the basket. Then she tucked the black stone carefully in. The moss sizzled and sent up tiny clouds of steam.

Hurry.

As if the bandits she'd dreamed up earlier were behind her, Mella scrambled along the path and back down the road toward the Inn. She couldn't run all the way, but she ran when she might, and in between bursts of speed she walked as briskly as she could. Otherwise someone might—

Might what?

Take the stone from her? Who would want it? Who would even know that she had it?

The logic of the question didn't loosen her grip on the basket or slow her steps. When she reached the Inn's yard, she hesitated. She couldn't see Mama, thank goodness. Poll, one of the stable boys, looked up.

"What's wrong then? Mella?"

Ignoring him, she hurried past. Da was talking to Atwin, standing with his mule and cart by the stable doors. He didn't see her. Across the yard, into the kitchen. If only Mama would be out . . .

She was. The kitchen was empty. Mella dashed up the stairs, past the second floor with the rooms for travelers, and up to the attic, where she slept with Lilla. Until last winter, Gran had slept there too, her bed on one side of the great stone chimney, the one Mella shared with Lilla on the other side.

Hardly thinking, Mella snatched a shawl off the end of her bed and wrapped it around the basket. She dropped flat on her stomach and tucked the bundle away beneath her bed, close to the chimney. The stone had been in the fire, after all. It might like the warmth, Mella thought vaguely. At any rate, it should be safe. No one would look for it there.

No one would take it from her.

Now to sneak out of the Inn again before Mama saw her and wanted to know why she was back so soon, and without the herbs she had been sent for.

As she hurried downstairs again, Mella could hear Mama on the second floor, talking to Raya, who came in to clean each day. Lilla was checking on the rising bread in the kitchen, so Mella lurked out of sight until her sister went back to the common room. Dashing out to the porch, she snatched up the egg-gathering basket. Da was still talking to Atwin by the stable, and now the boy Roger was there too, and his master, Damien. Roger held the reins of a fine chestnut gelding. Mella aimed to slip past, keeping the squire and his horse between herself and Da. Then on to the gate and the road, and she'd be safe.

What *was* that sound?

It came out of the forest, something between a roar and a howl, and it rose and fell like the wind on a stormy night. All across the yard heads lifted, and talk ceased. The dragons hissed and chattered wildly, dashing around their pen in a flurry of flapping wings and lashing tails. Automatically Mella turned toward her herd, meaning to calm them. But they quieted themselves a moment later and crowded up against the fence, necks stretched long, eyes wide, listening.

"A hunting cat," Da said loudly as Roger petted and soothed the chestnut horse, which fidgeted anxiously and rolled its eyes.

"Cats hunt at night," Atwin said uneasily, looking around as if the thing that had howled might pounce on him.

"An eagle, then," Da answered him shortly.

Her father was right, Mella thought, trying to make her heart settle back down where it belonged. There were plenty of creatures in the forest who might make a sound like that. Weren't there? Echoes did strange things to noises, she told herself firmly, ducking around behind Da to get to the gate. It need not have been anything dire or dreadful.

She could not stop thinking, however, that something about that cry had been familiar. Loss, that had been it. It was a cry someone who had lost something precious might make.

And as she shut the Inn's gate behind her, she caught a glimpse of Damien standing very still, upright, not stirring even as Roger brought his horse, now calm, to his side. The fingers of one hand lightly touched the pendant around his neck. *He* didn't look as if he'd lost something. On the contrary, he looked as if he'd found what he'd spent his life searching for.

Mella was tired by the time she reached the cave. After all, she'd already walked the distance twice that morning and run it once. With a sigh, she sat down by the stream, picked up Cate's provisions from where she'd left them, and packed them away in the egg-gathering basket.

Goodness, that cave smelled of sulfur. And smoke as well. Had she left that fire burning when she'd rescued the stone from it?

And what was that—over *there*? A flash of wet scarlet caught her eye. Turning her head, Mella found herself looking at the dead body of a deer, huddled against an earthen bank. Its coat was the same soft brown as the dirt, which was why she hadn't seen it at first, until the blood on its throat had sprung into her sight.

The blood was still wet. Fresh. Had someone been hunting? But no arrow had made that gaping wound in the deer's throat.

And had there always been that boulder near the mouth of the cave? It was huge, towering well over Mella's head. How had she never noticed it before?

Something rushed snakelike along the ground at Mella's feet. With a yelp she jumped up. She hadn't seen the thing itself, only the movement, and she spun around looking for it.

The voice that spoke behind her was deep, and it echoed as though it came from the bottom of a well. It sounded old, as old as stone. A wild thought sparked in Mella's mind. It sounded as though the mountain itself were speaking.

And what it spoke was a single word.

"Thief!"

Something long and smooth whipped around Mella's waist, and her feet were lifted off the ground, so quickly that she had no time even to scream. Not that screaming would have done her much good, Mella thought, as she was turned around in midair. Not when she was looking into a long, narrow face covered in fine scales. A wash of color spread over the scales, changing them from the dull gray of weather-beaten stone to the pale green of lichen. Wisps of steam curled from flaring nostrils.

The boy, Roger, had been wrong. Mella's father had been wrong. There *were* dragons.

It was a pity she would not live long enough to tell them so.

The dragon, holding Mella in midair, stepped away from the tumbled slope of rocks near the mouth of the cave. Now that it was no longer trying to hide, the natural color of its scales swept across the body and down the long neck crowned with the large, bristling crest that told Mella this dragon was a male, and a very angry one. Ignoring the dead deer at his feet, he kept dark brown eyes, flecked with gold, fixed on Mella. Perhaps he didn't like venison, Mella thought, dizzy with terror. Perhaps he only ate deer when he couldn't get human.

More steam escaped as the dragon opened his mouth to speak. A little whimpering sound crawled out of Mella's throat at the sight of the long white fangs.

"Where is it?" the dragon demanded. "I smell it on you. Where have you taken it? Speak!"

But Mella could not. Fear trapped her tongue, made her heart pound in her chest like the black-smith's hammer on the anvil. And the tail around her waist was cruelly tight, cutting off her breath.

"Speak!" the dragon repeated, drawing out the *S* in a long hiss.

"I don't know," Mella gasped, shutting her eyes. It was easier to get words out if she couldn't see that face, those eyes, those teeth. "I don't know what—what you mean—I—"

"Do not lie!" the dragon thundered. "You have stolen the Egg. I can smell it!"

The black stone. Like an egg in a nest of fire.

"Oh," she whispered politely, feebly. "Was that . . . yours? I didn't know—"

"Thief! Where have you taken it?"

"I'm not a thief!" This time Mella didn't gasp. She yelled. And she opened her eyes.

Dragons can smell fear, Gran had always said. A keeper lets them know who's in charge.

This . . . this *thing* that towered as tall as the highest oak and talked like the mountain speaking—this thing was a dragon. And Mella was a keeper.

She would not let him call her a thief.

The tail around her middle loosened just a little. It was hard to read much expression on a face covered with scales. But she thought the dragon looked . . . surprised.

"A black egg?" she asked. "As heavy as stone?"

The long, narrow nostrils quivered with rage or impatience or anxiety. The huge head nodded.

"I *found* it," Mella said, glaring. "I didn't *steal* it. And I'll tell you where it is. If you *put—me—down.*"

Nothing happened for a long moment.

Then, very slowly, the dragon lowered Mella to the ground and unwrapped its tail from her waist.

Mella's knees were as wobbly as water. Luckily

there was a fair-size boulder behind her. When she sat down on that, it was not as obvious as if she'd collapsed on the ground.

"Where?" the dragon growled, low but fierce. His tail twitched where it lay along the ground, close enough to snatch Mella up again in an instant.

"It's at the Inn," Mella said as steadily as she could. "I'll fetch it for you. But you have to leave. At *once*."

The dragon laughed. The sound made Mella's skin crawl as if it wanted to go somewhere and hide. She had to clench her hands into fists to keep from clapping them over her ears.

Wings unfolded from the dragon's back, batlike wings with pale gray green skin stretched between long ribs. One of those wings had a tear in the fragile skin, the edges of it rough with dark, dried blood. Had the injury been made by the arrow of a hunter from Grimsby? Was that what had brought the dragon to hide in this cave so near humans?

The dragon's head, larger than a horse's, swooped down close to Mella's face. She couldn't hold back a shriek and squeezed her eyes closed so that she wouldn't have to look at the white teeth, each longer than her finger, the snaky tongue, and the deep red throat as the dragon opened his mouth.

Steam tickled her neck. What a fool she'd been to think that she could cow this dragon, stare him down, make him listen to her. She wasn't Gran. She wasn't and would never be the kind of keeper who could do that.

Any moment now those sharp teeth would tear deep into her, and she would look like the deer, huddled on the ground in death. Let it be quick, she prayed. Please. Please.

The dragon's voice rumbled in her bones.

"Do you tell me what to do, little human child? I will burn this Inn to the ground and pluck the Egg from its ashes!"

"No!" Mella shouted uselessly, her eyes springing open again. "You can't!"

But of course the dragon could and would. He laughed at her again. Her mother, her father, Lilla, even Roger and his master—

"You can't!" she cried triumphantly. "There's a dragon-slayer there!"

The dragon paused. His wings quivered slightly. "A Defender?"

"Yes!" Mella hardly noticed that she'd jumped to her feet. "With weapons and armor." Well, Damien's packs and saddlebags *had* been very heavy. She remembered her father grumbling as he'd dragged them up the stairs. "He'll kill you if you come near."

"Just one Defender." The dragon's tail lashed and in one quick movement uprooted a spruce sapling to Mella's left. Her stomach did a queasy roll as she saw the spike on the tail's end, as long as her forearm and as sharp as a butcher's knife. "One is not so many."

"There are two," Mella said quickly. After all, if Roger was a squire, he'd be a knight someday.

The dragon snorted. The claws of one forefoot raked deep furrows in the earth.

"But I'll get the egg for you," Mella promised. "I
know where it is. I'll get it and bring it, if you wait
here for me."

"You will give the alarm to this Defender," the
dragon said, staring at Mella. "You will call out all
your village to hunt me down."

"I won't," Mella promised. "My word."

"Humans have no honor," the dragon growled.
"How can I trust your word?"

"I don't lie," Mella insisted, grateful for the
anger that stiffened her spine and steadied her
voice. "I'm not a liar. I'm not a thief. I'll do what I
say. But you must promise too. To go away with
your egg. To hurt no one here."

The dragon looked suspiciously at Mella with
one brown eye and then the other.

"You know where the Egg is, you say? It is safe?"

Mella nodded. "Wrapped in my shawl. Close to
the chimney."

"Foolish human!" Steam blew in Mella's face. "The Egg must be kept warm. It must lie in fire. Cold will kill it!"

"I'll fetch it now," Mella offered quickly. "But I won't go until you promise."

The dragon closed one eye. He was thinking.

"Do not imagine," he said slowly, "that one Defender frightens me. Or two, even." The brown eye opened again. "But the Egg must be kept safe. If I am injured again, if I cannot fly, then all is lost." The dragon's head nodded slowly, heavily. "If you keep your side of this bargain, so will I."

Mella nodded. She stood up straight, brushed dirt and spruce needles from the back of her skirt, and turned to walk down the path, trying to look as if she were not quivering all over with a mixture of fear and relief.

"Wait!" The dragon's tail crashed down in front of her, blocking the way. Twigs and acorns went flying. "If you lie to me, human, then I will not stay to fight the Defenders. I will fly to my home. My wing is strong enough for that. But I will return, and with more of my kind. Then every house here will be burned to the ground. No one will escape. Do you understand, little human thief?"

Mella swallowed.

"I'm *not* a thief," she said. "And I understand."

The dragon lifted his tail. Mella ran.

Chapter Four

"Mella Evasdaughter!"

Mama stood with her hands on her hips, looking down at her younger child.

"Mama, listen—" Mella tried to say between gasps.

She had run all the way back to the Inn, only to arrive breathless, with her braid undone, her skirt muddy, and her basket gone. Her mother had not been pleased.

"Where is the basket? Where are the herbs I sent you for? What have you been doing this long time? Well, girl?"

"Mama, there was—"

"Never mind! I don't want to hear it. Playing

some game in the woods, forgetting your errand, losing good food—you're too old for such foolishness. Lilla can go to Cate's this afternoon, and you can scrub every inch of the kitchen floor. Perhaps that'll teach you not to be so careless."

"But, Mama!"

"*What,* child?" Mama's cheeks were bright red, her eyes narrow. And Mella's words died on her tongue.

If she said there was a dragon hidden in the woods, her mother would think it nothing but a fairy story, and Mella would only lose her supper as well as being forced to scrub the kitchen floor. And if, by some miracle, her mother believed her, what would she do but tell Damien, the dragon-slayer? *Then every house here will be burned to the ground,* the dragon had said. *No one will escape.*

"Nothing, Mama."

Mella's mother let out her breath in a long sigh through tight lips. "Then get you into the kitchen and start scrubbing."

Mella had no chance even to slip upstairs to the

attic and make sure the egg was safe under her bed, for Mama was shaping the risen bread dough into loaves while keeping an eye on Mella's work. On her hands and knees, skirts tucked up, Mella scrubbed her way inch by inch across the stone floor and worried. Would the dragon wait? Would the egg grow too cold? The kitchen floor had never seemed so big. Surely it was *miles* across. If Mama would only finish with her baking, Mella could sneak out, seize the egg, and run. No matter what her punishment would be afterward.

"There now!" Mama set the loaves into the warming cupboard, built into the wall beside the chimney, to rise a second time. Mella put her head down and worked the brush industriously across the floor as Mama washed her hands, dried them on her apron, and left the kitchen.

Now! Mella dropped the brush into the bucket and jumped up, just as Mama came back from the cold room with a cheese in her hands. Mella pretended to be stretching her back, and Mama, with a sniff, began to slice up the cheese.

The brush rasped across the stones. The soapy water was cold and harsh on Mella's hands. Mama would *never* be done slicing that cheese! But she finished at last and went up to the second floor. Mella crept to the foot of the stairs and stood listening. She heard Mama talking to Raya. They must be standing together on the second-floor landing. No hope that Mella could creep around them and fetch the egg.

In desperation, Mella looked around the kitchen for an idea, and caught a glimpse of green ribbons in fair hair through the door to the common room.

"Lilla!" Mella whispered as loudly as she dared.

"What is it?" Coming to the doorway, Lilla crossed her arms and looked unfriendly.

"Lilla, please," Mella begged. "I need something from our room."

"Get it yourself."

"I'm meant to be scrubbing the floor. If Mama sees me . . ."

Lilla sniffed. "Next time you want a favor from me, perhaps you'll keep your tongue off me and

Jonas Evadson. I'm not putting myself out for *you.*" She turned and walked away just as Mella heard footsteps coming down the stairs. When Mama came in she was scrubbing again.

Mama went to the cold room once more and came back. To the stables and came back. To the common room and came back. Mella could have wept with frustration. But when Mama went out on the porch to talk to Da, she saw another chance.

She had scrubbed her way over to the common room door, and in the other room she heard a whistled tune. A plan formed in her mind.

"Roger!" she called softly.

The squire, a small book in his hand, stopped and lifted his eyebrows as he looked at her. Mella was sorry now that she'd been so short with him before, but there was no help for it.

"Please," she whispered at him. "I need you."

Knights had to help when they were asked, didn't they? And squires too. Mella thought so. After a moment, Roger came over to the doorway.

Mella wasted no time. "Up in the attic. The

stairs over there." She pointed with her chin. "There's a basket wrapped up in a shawl under the bed. Bring it to me."

Roger stared down at her, puzzled. "But what is it? Why do you need it?"

"Just go now," Mella insisted. She hated to grovel like this, on her knees before him. But she would, if it could save the egg and the Inn. "Please," she begged. "I've no one else to ask."

Roger hesitated for a moment. Then, tucking his book into a pocket, he crossed the kitchen and disappeared up the stairs just as Mama came back from the porch.

Roger had the sense not to come down until Mama had left the room again. But the instant she was gone he hurried into the kitchen with the basket in one hand. "What *is* it?" he demanded. "It's heavy as a rock!"

"*Careful* with it!" Tugging her gloves on, Mella anxiously lifted the egg from the basket. It was definitely less hot than it had been earlier, but she was relieved still to feel some warmth through the dragonhide. "Make a place in the coals for it," she ordered Roger.

The look on Roger's face told her that he would not do much more for her without an explanation. But he picked up the poker and dug a hole in the red and black coals in the hearth. Gingerly Mella tucked the egg down into its fiery nest and raked coals over it so that it was hidden.

"What is it?" Roger asked again. "It felt like a stone, but so hot! What keeps heat like that?"

"I can't tell you." Mella knew how churlish she must seem. He had helped her, when all she'd been was rude to him. But he was the dragon-slayer's squire. How could she tell him he had just helped to save a dragon's egg?

And suddenly it occurred to her that he could help with something else as well. "Where's your master?" she asked.

"Damien? He went out. He heard something in the woods—well, you were there, you heard it too. And what do you mean, you can't tell me? I helped you!"

Mella could hardly blame Roger for being exasperated. But at least the egg was warm again. Now, if only the dragon had the sense to stay hidden, so that Damien wouldn't find him . . .

"Listen," Roger began, but something stopped him.

It was the sound of Lilla screaming.

Mella, with Roger on her heels, raced out into the Inn's yard. Her heart pounding, she looked up, scanning the skies for the dragon. It must have become tired of waiting for her or decided that she was not trustworthy and come to take its egg for itself.

But there was nothing in the air. She brought her gaze down and saw the chestnut horse turning in from the road.

Damien was slumped over his steed's neck. Roger was beside him now and caught him, or tried to, as his master tumbled from the saddle. But they both would have ended up in a heap on the ground if Mella's father hadn't run to help. "Lilla! Fetch a healer," Da bellowed. "Help me with him, let's get him to a bed." Peder and Poll, the stable boys, ran forward, along with a few of the guests. Mella retreated into the kitchen as, with Roger leading the way, they carried Damien inside and up the stairs. His eyes were closed; blood dripped from his forehead. There was blood elsewhere, as well. Too much of it. He had on a leather coat with metal plates sewn into its length; the steel had been blackened as if with fire, and some of the plates were torn. Mella could too easily imagine the claws and teeth that could rip steel as though it were the thinnest, finest linen.

Roger, white faced, ran down the stairs again and through the common room out into the yard. Mella was left alone in the kitchen. It was strangely quiet.

I will return, and with more of my kind.

The dragon must think she'd broken her word and sent Damien to kill it. She had to prove that it wasn't so. If there were the slightest chance that the dragon had not left yet . . .

Her gloves protecting her hands, she burrowed through the coals in the hearth to snatch up the egg. A crowd was gathering in the Inn's yard, but no one noticed Mella as she ran. Bits of conversation trailed after her.

"It could not have been a dragon."

"Indeed it was, looks like it bit his leg clean off—"

"—dying now—"

"But did he kill it?"

"Where is it?"

That was the question indeed, Mella thought, as she rounded the corner of the stable and ran straight into Roger.

Chapter Five

Mella didn't fall down, but she staggered back. Instinctively she hugged the egg close to her body to protect it. Roger, knocked against the stable wall, blinked at her. He had a saddlebag in one hand; he must have been sent to fetch something for Damien.

"What are you doing?" He stared at her. "Where are you taking that—that thing? Wait!"

No time, no time, Mella thought, and she dashed around him. He grabbed at her sleeve but missed.

"There's a *dragon* out there! A true one! Wait!"

Mella ran her fastest. The egg, clutched close to her stomach, was warm enough to fight the icy fear that seemed to seep out from her heart. Too late. She would be too late. And it would not only be Damien who died. The Inn, the village, everyone she knew . . .

Her heart was hammering against her ribs, and her breath was coming in huge, loud gasps by the time she left the main road for the side path. Her braid snagged on a branch, but she jerked it loose without looking back and kept going. Up the bank, over the stream to the cave, just as she had twice already that morning . . .

No dragon.

But there was a wide swath beaten through the undergrowth. A dead bush still smoldered. Black cinders crunched under Mella's feet. With difficulty, holding the egg in one hand, she climbed over the trunk of a tree torn up from the earth, clods of soft dirt still clinging to its roots. Sliding awkwardly down the other side, she saw the dragon.

He lay in a little clearing, his scales now dull and gray. The long neck snaked along the ground, the head half hidden in the grass. A spear was buried a foot deep in the breast.

Mella stood on the edge of the clearing. She should have been glad. The dragon-slayer had succeeded. The beast that had threatened her and her family was dead.

Dead like Gran. Dead like Lady.

Blinking back tears, Mella made her way across the grass and knelt by the dragon's head. Her hair had come loose from its braid and tumbled down around her face. Why should she feel grief? He had been so . . . alive, that was all. Beautiful, with those gray green scales and eyes like sunlight on the surface of a deep, dark well. Terrifying, but beautiful. And she had made him a promise.

"I brought your egg," she said aloud. "I didn't tell him where to find you. I kept my word."

One of the dragon's eyelids lifted.

Mella gasped. But the dragon didn't move.

"A human with honor." The dragon's voice was a creaky whisper. "Can this be?"

"Here." Mella held out the egg. "I brought it. It's safe."

The dragon sighed. His tongue, the color of

blood mixed with ash, flicked out to touch the egg briefly.

"Small human." The brown eye, darker than before, held Mella's gaze. "I have failed."

Just as before, it was hard to read much expression on a face covered with scales. But no one could have missed the bitterness in the dragon's voice.

No, Mella wanted to say. *You tried. You did your best.*

But she knew—she'd found out since Gran had died—that trying your best didn't mean you wouldn't fail.

"You," the dragon whispered. "You have the Egg now."

"I'll take care of it," Mella said softly. "I promise."

"Keep it warm." The words came slowly, between painful pauses for breath. "It must be placed in fire every night."

Mella nodded. The dragon's eye closed.

"Wait!" Mella leaned forward. "Will another dragon come for it? How long should I keep it?"

"No." The dragon heaved in a long, difficult breath. His injured wing, lying limp on the grass, quivered with the effort. "There is not time. To wait for another. You must take the Egg home."

"Home?" Mella pictured the egg hatching in the Inn's courtyard. She tried to imagine a dragon the size of the one before her sharing the pen with the Inn's herd.

"From the human's town," the dragon whispered. "Follow the river. Look for the waterfall. Above, two matching peaks. The Fangs. Between them is the Hatching Ground. The Egg must hatch there. Less than a day's flight from here."

"Into the *mountains*!" Mella nearly dropped the egg. "I can't—I never—"

"You have promised!" The dragon's head, trembling with effort, lifted from the grass. Mella could have wept to see the pain the movement caused.

The dragon's head wavered on its neck. Its eyes held Mella. They seemed to be growing darker by the second. Mella felt as if they were drawing her forward and down.

"A human with honor," the dragon growled. "You have promised."

But not this, Mella wanted to cry. *I never promised this!*

So you think you can be a keeper, do you? Gran's voice suddenly rang in Mella's ears. *It's no light thing you're taking on, my girl. A keeper must see to the dragons every day, in all weathers. You'll sit up with the sick ones, look after the chicks. Dragons are uncanny beasts. They'll take to some and not others. No question, they've taken to you, ever since you were a little toddling thing. But now you must live up to your part of the bargain. You must take care of them.*

She was a keeper. She had promised.

The Egg burned in Mella's hands. Without noticing, she began to think of it as the dragon had spoken of it. Not as an egg, but as the Egg.

"I will," Mella said softly.

The dragon laid his head down again with a long sigh. Something slithered and rustled in the grass. It was the dragon's tail. The sharp tip lifted and, very gently, brushed against Mella's cheek.

"Good flying," the dragon murmured, his voice very faint now. "May the wind rise beneath your wings."

"I don't have wings," Mella objected.

The dragon didn't answer.

Mella sat back on her heels, holding tightly to the Egg. What had she done? Had the dragon laid a spell on her, to make her agree so easily to carry the Egg into the Dragontooth Mountains? It was madness. She was only twelve years old. She could never do such a thing alone.

"Are you really going?"

The voice came from behind her back.

Trying to jump up, turn around, and hold on to the Egg at the same time didn't work. Mella fell over onto the grass and wriggled up into a sitting position, staring at Roger. He was standing not ten yards away. All her attention must have been on the dragon, and his on her, to have missed the sound of his approach.

"You followed me!"

Roger was shaking his head slowly. "That's a

dragon," he said. "A real one. A true dragon."

"Of course it is." Mella found that there were tears on her cheeks. She brushed them off with one hand, holding the Egg with the other.

"*Look* at it." Slowly, step by step, Roger came closer. "I never thought—I didn't know—it's *real.*"

It's dead, Mella wanted to shout. *It's real and it's dead. Because of your master.*

But she couldn't. What would Roger do? Run home and tell everyone at the Inn that he'd heard her talking to a dragon?

She had to convince him somehow not to tell. She had to coax the dragon-slayer's squire into helping her save a dragon's egg.

"Roger, listen—"

Roger didn't seem to hear her.

"That wingspan," he marveled. "It must be twenty feet. Still, it's heavy. How does it get airborne? Does it have hollow bones, like a bird's?"

Mella gaped at him.

"And it *talked* to you." Roger dropped to his

knees beside Mella and the dragon. "I heard it."

"It's not my fault. I was just trying to—"

"But its mouth, its tongue—they're not shaped for speech. At least not human speech. How could it talk?"

Mella had a question of her own. *Why aren't you angry?* Roger's eyes were wide, his face eager. Why did the dragon-slayer's squire look like he thought a dragon was a wintertide gift?

But she didn't dare ask. No sense reminding Roger that he should have been furious.

"Can they really breathe fire?" Roger went on. His hand, hesitating a little, gingerly stroked the smooth scales on the dragon's neck.

"I don't know," Mella admitted. "I think it did, back there. . . ." She waved a hand at the trail of trampled undergrowth and scorched trees. "The common ones can only snort a little steam."

"Really?" Roger looked fascinated. "I wonder how closely they're related. Do you think—"

"Why did you follow me?" Mella broke in. She hadn't meant to interrupt, to be rude. But she didn't understand this, the way Roger was maundering on.

"Your healer's with Damien. She sent me out of the room." Roger looked a little embarrassed. "I don't like blood much. And I remembered which way you'd gone, with that—that thing. I found this in the hedge—" He held out her red hair ribbon, and his eyes dropped to the Egg. "That's a dragon's egg."

Mella nodded. "I found it. This morning." *Thief!* the dragon had roared at her. But she hadn't meant to steal. She hadn't known. "It was hunting, I think." The dead deer, its bloody throat. "It had to leave the Egg alone. And I . . ."

If she hadn't found the Egg, if she hadn't taken it, would the dragon, once it had eaten, have been on its way? Then it would not be dead, and Mella would not have the Egg in her hands and the responsibility for its fate weighing on her. And Damien would have found nothing to fight. That made two deaths on her conscience. Two more.

"Well, then." Roger looked thoughtful. "We

have to get it to the Hatching Ground, don't you think? How much time do we have?"

"We?" Mella stared at Roger. To her astonishment, he blushed.

"I mean . . . if you don't mind my coming?"

Mella was not usually at a loss for words, but she couldn't figure out how to answer. Mind? She didn't mind, precisely. Just a moment ago she had thought that she could never do this alone. Mind? That wasn't it.

This didn't make sense. She was a keeper, she'd talked to the dragon, she'd made a promise. Mella knew why *she* meant to save the Egg. But Roger . . .

"Why would you want to?" she demanded. "It's a dragon! They said your master's dying. It killed him!"

"Damien's not dead," Roger answered, although his face grew sober. "The healer said he should recover, if he doesn't take fever too badly. And anyway, it was just defending its young. Any living thing would do the same. You can't blame it for that."

Mella shook her head, bewildered.

"It's a true dragon," Roger went on, and his face lit up with excitement. "I never thought they were real. Can you imagine, seeing one up close? *Talking* to it? Well, you can, I suppose. Imagine. I mean, you don't need to. But I . . ." His eyes traveled over the bulk of the dragon, its torn wing, its blood-stained breast. "It's *magnificent*. We have to take care of that egg. You'll let me come?"

Mella didn't know what to answer.

Chapter Six

Mella perched on the saddle behind Roger, clinging to his waist. Her skirts were gathered up above her knees, which made her blush. But no one could see her red cheeks in the dark. And she didn't dare sit sidesaddle, or she'd slide right off the horse's back and land in the dirt.

It would have been more comfortable if they'd taken Damien's horse as well as Roger's. Mella had wanted to, but Roger had refused. "That's *stealing*," he'd said, his freckled face shocked in the dim yellow light of the lantern.

Mella didn't think so. They would return the horse in a few days, after all, and it wasn't as if Damien could ride it at the moment. But she couldn't put up much of an argument when they could only speak in whispers for fear that Peder and Poll, asleep in the loft overhead, would hear. So they had only Roger's gray mare, not Damien's chestnut gelding.

Roger set the horse to a steady jog, heading east to Dragonsford. Mella yawned. The long day had taken a toll on her. She had struggled to keep awake as she lay in bed, waiting for Lilla to fall asleep so she could sneak outside unnoticed. Now, despite the chill of the night air, her eyes kept drifting shut. She forced them open again, with an effort, and discovered that her cheek had come to rest against Roger's shoulders.

She sat bolt upright.

Roger had pulled the horse to a halt. "Far enough?" he said over his shoulder. "There's a bit of a clearing there."

"Far enough," Mella agreed, stifling another yawn. Their plan had been simply to get away from the Inn tonight, and tomorrow morning ride the rest of the way to Dragonsford.

Tomorrow morning. Mella couldn't stop thinking of that, even while she gathered a few sticks
and fallen branches, groping about in the brambles and roots at the edge of the clearing. Roger
was taking care of the horse, removing the saddle
and bridle.

Tomorrow morning Mella's parents would
wake, and she would be gone. They would be
frantic. Guilt clutched at Mella's heart. They
would search the woods. They would call in all the
village to help. Would they think she'd been kidnapped? That she'd run away with Roger? Would
they think another dragon had eaten her?

And her own dragons. Da would have to pay
coin that the Inn could ill afford and hire Tilda
from the village to look after them, a keeper too
old now for a herd of her own. But they'd be restless and unhappy without Mella. A herd was
never right when the keeper was not there.

Mella wished she'd been able at least to leave
her family a note. Her father could read and write
well enough to keep the Inn's accounts. He would

have been able to puzzle out a message. But Mella had never learned writing. Too late, it occurred to her that Roger was probably lettered. Wasn't that something squires had to learn? She could have asked for his help. But there was no point in dwelling on it now.

She'd be home again as quickly as she could. The dragon had said the Hatching Ground was less than a day's flight away. It might take a bit longer on horseback. But surely her parents and her dragons would only have two or three days to miss her.

Something rustled in the darkness between the trees. Paws or a tail raked through dry leaves and dead twigs. Mella jumped a little.

"What's that?" Roger asked. Finished with the horse, he'd come to stand at her elbow.

"I don't know." It might be almost anything. A badger. A fox. Not big or heavy enough to be a bear. A snake, even. Mella's toes twitched in her shoes.

Then a breeze drifted across her face, and she

caught a hint of a familiar, dry, sulfury smell.

"Dragons," she told Roger. "Wild dragons."

"Oh?" Roger looked excited. "They're rare. Have you seen them before?"

"Not really," Mella admitted. The wild common dragons were shy and came out to hunt at night, so she had only caught a glimpse or two, now and then, in the twilight forest—a scaled flank or snout behind shadowy leaves, a tail slithering through the grass.

Now she seemed to hear rustling from all sides. A hiss teased at her ears as she turned, with a shiver, to pile her firewood in a heap at the center of the clearing. It wasn't as if she was afraid of the little wild dragons. Of course not. Still, she felt better when Roger had struck a spark and, after much puffing and blowing, had a fire burning. She was glad as much for the cheerful light as for the warmth.

"Are they related?" Roger asked as Mella found her cloak and her dragonhide gloves inside the sack she'd brought from the Inn.

"Who?" Gloves on, Mella dug into the sack again and drew out the metal box her mother kept candles in. It now held the Egg. "Wild dragons and tame ones? Aye, they're practically the same." She wondered, as she flipped up the catch and opened the lid of the box, who the first keeper had been. Who'd first coaxed a shy wild dragon out of a thicket or a cave, fed it, learned to rub behind its ears the way dragons liked? Who'd been the first to *know*, deep in her bones, when a herd was hungry or frightened or threatened with sickness?

"No, I meant—well, that's interesting too. But the true dragons. Like that one today. Are they related to the wild ones?"

How could Mella know something like that? She lifted the Egg out of the coals she had packed around it and settled it in the heat of Roger's fire, realizing as she did that Roger had not expected her to answer at all. He went on talking.

"It's hard to think so. But the true ones *look* like your farm dragons, you have to admit. The neck, and the tail with its spike, and the shape of the head. The wings are larger in the big ones, of course. . . ."

Mella stopped listening. Knees under her chin, she watched the Egg, wrapped in flame like a baby in a blanket. It had seemed dull as coal when she'd lifted it out of the box, but now, as it warmed, colors began to swirl again across its surface. Or underneath it, rather. It was as if the black shell grew translucent in the heat and let her catch a glimpse of the Egg's heart.

After a while she noticed that Roger had stopped talking. He was looking at her expectantly. "Have you always known?" he asked, and she realized that he was repeating the question.

"Known what?"

"That you wanted to be a keeper."

Mella smiled. "Always. When I was barely old enough to walk, my parents found me asleep in the dragons' pen. They were afraid I'd be killed, but the dragons just curled up around me and watched over me. That's when Gran knew. . . ."

"Knew what?"

"She said I had the touch. She taught me."

"Your grandmother was a keeper?"

"The best in the kingdom," Mella answered proudly, despite the tightness in her throat. Gran had been skinny and tough and gnarled like an old oak root, and she could make a dragon obey her at a look. "People came for miles around for her help if a herd was sick or if they wanted advice on breeding. Gran knew everything."

Everything.

Even before Mella had opened her eyes, she'd known.

The herd was still asleep, huddled together as they always were, sharing the warmth of their scaly bodies. She'd felt them, a knot of limbs and tails and wings. It was not a dream, something that skimmed lightly over the surface of her sleeping mind. It was deeper than that; it lodged itself firmly under her breastbone, next to her beating heart. Her dragons would always be there.

You look after them now, girl.

"Yes, Gran," Mella mumbled sleepily. She pushed back the heavy winter quilt and stuck her feet out of the bed. Lilla moaned as an icy draft snaked its way under the blankets.

"Mella, what *are* you doing?"

"Feed the dragons," Mella muttered stupidly. The rag rug beside the bed was nearly as cold as the bare wooden floor.

"*What?* Mella, it's the middle of the night. You're dreaming."

Indeed, it was dark. No moonlight came through the one window in the far wall. It seemed as if the floor, the dresses and shawls hanging on the wall and the shoes beneath them, Gran in her bed on the other side of the chimney, had all vanished.

"*Mella*. You're letting the cold in."

Mella hesitated. "Gran?"

Lilla was right. It was the heart of night. It was no time to bring scraps and fresh meat out to the dragons. But why had Gran spoken to her then?

"She's asleep. Honestly, Mella, I think you are too. Get back in bed."

Mella did. She would have to check on Blackie's wing in the morning, she thought. Her own shoulder ached a little, and she rubbed it absently. He'd caught his wing on a nail, tearing the thin, tender skin. She'd have to make sure it didn't get infected. Keep it clean, that was the key. Gran would help her. Even a sick or injured dragon was patient under Gran's soothing hands.

But Gran didn't help her in the morning. Gran didn't wake again. Mella, trying to keep Blackie quiet while she smoothed salve over the cut on his wing, remembered the words she'd heard in the night.

"I will, Gran," she whispered. "I promise."

And now she'd left them. Run away with a knight's squire and a dragon's egg and left them behind.

And it wasn't the first time she'd broken her promise to Gran. Barely a week after Gran had gone, there had been Lady.

"What about you?" she asked Roger quickly.

"Why did you become a Defender? You didn't even believe in dragons."

She saw a flash of white as Roger smiled. "I suppose I was wrong about that. But I thought there might be, when I first became a squire. Maybe not giant ones, fire-breathers. But something, some fact behind the legend. Some reason for all the old stories. And it was better than . . ."

Mella felt sleepiness creeping up on her. But she was curious too. "Better than what?" A yawn nearly swallowed the last word.

"Learning to fight. My brothers are all squires to military orders. My oldest brother died at the attack on Tyrene. Siege tactics and fortifications and hacking people to pieces . . . At least with the Defenders I got to be outdoors. They're always traveling the borderlands and the mountains, looking for signs of dragons. My father wasn't pleased."

"Why not?"

"He thought it was foolishness, taking an oath to keep the kingdom safe from dragons. He says the Defenders are a relic, out of date. He said I made the family look ridiculous and I should join a military order, too. Get myself killed, like Aliard."

Mella felt another yawn forcing its way up her throat. Her eyelids were getting heavy. Roger's voice was gentle and sad.

Mella lay down on her side, wrapping herself in her cloak, staring into the fire, now settling itself into a small heap of red orange coals with the Egg glowing black at its heart. She was sorry about Roger's brother. She thought she should tell him so, but she fell asleep instead.

Chapter Seven

In her dreams, Mella was missing something.

Gran?

No, not her grandmother. Someone else. There was a gap, like an ache in the air, where something had been taken.

What was it? It was hard for her to say. It was as if someone had stolen her liver or her kidney, something that had always been inside her, so much a part of her that she never thought about it at all. Now it was gone and nothing would be right with her until whatever was gone had returned.

Restless, she squirmed in her sleep, twisting her cloak around herself. But the wrongness couldn't be solved that way. With something other than her ears she heard a whimper and a long, low, hungry howl that shivered its way down into her bones.

When Mella woke, still tired, her cloak was damp with dew. Her nose felt like a frozen lump clinging to her face, and her tears made her cheeks even colder.

It had been no dream. She had felt her dragons missing her.

A herd was always restless without its keeper. Oh, Tilda would feed them and keep an eye out for injuries or sickness. But they'd pine for Mella the way Lady had pined for Gran.

Gran had never left the herd, not even for a day. Other keepers did, when trips to the market or the city had to be made. There were even itinerant keepers with no herds of their own who made their way from town to town, offering to care for dragons so that their keepers could rest or travel.

Poor, pitiful things, Gran had called those gypsy keepers. Wastrels and wanderers. She wouldn't trust her dragons to one of them for a day. A keeper with no herd of her own was no true keeper.

But Gran had left her dragons after all. And now Mella had done the same. No. Not the same. She would be back. But how could you tell a dragon that? How could she have let her herd know that she was not abandoning them for good?

But what else could she have done, caught between a promise to her dying grandmother and a promise to a dying dragon?

The Egg!

The thought of it pulled Mella bolt upright. Careless, she reached a bare hand into the ashes of the fire and snatched it back a second later. Sucking her burned finger, she sighed with relief. The Egg had not cooled.

Roger was stirring. Before he could wake entirely, Mella retreated into the woods to take care of her own most pressing need. When she returned she found that Roger had gotten up too. Kneeling by the fire, he had a spruce twig thick with needles in his hand and had brushed away the coals and ashes that Mella had heaped over the Egg. Now it was half exposed to the chilly morning air.

"What are you *doing*?"

Roger turned to look up at Mella, surprised. "Just . . . checking on it. It's all right, it hasn't cooled, see—"

"It'll get cold! What are you thinking?"

"It's still in the fire."

"It needs to be covered!" Snatching up her gloves, Mella hurriedly packed the Egg away in the metal box, cushioning it with ashes that would hold in its natural heat until she could put it in a fire once more.

"I only wanted—" Roger started to say.

"Well, don't," Mella answered tartly as she latched the lid of the box. "I'm the keeper. I'll look after the Egg. You just—"

Mella didn't finish the sentence because she couldn't think, exactly, of what Roger should do. This was *her* quest. She may have left her dragons behind, and she may have been unable to save

Lady, but she *would* take care of the Egg. The dragon had laid it on her to do so. Roger had just . . . happened to be there.

He might be useful enough in one way or another. But he shouldn't meddle with the Egg. That was her concern, not his.

Packing the box away in her sack, Mella refused to feel remorse for her sharp words or for the slump in Roger's shoulders. They shared the food Mella had brought from the Inn's kitchen: hard traveler's bread, some apples, a chunk of cheese. It was a quiet meal.

"We should go," Roger said after they had finished. He seemed willing to forget that they had more or less quarreled. "If they come searching for us . . ." He didn't finish the sentence but tossed the core of his apple away into the woods and rose to saddle the mare.

"I hope Damien's all right," he muttered anxiously as he tightened the girth. "I'm supposed to look after him."

"My parents will take care of him." Mella tried

to make her voice gentle, to show that as long as Roger did not interfere with the Egg she could be as civil as anyone. And then she wished she could stop thinking about her parents, waking to find her gone. At first they would think she was out with the dragons. How long before they realized she was truly missing, and Roger too?

"My father always says once you've decided what you must do, nothing else matters." Roger looked a little doubtful of this wisdom. "And we have to do this. Don't we?"

Mella felt the weight of the Egg in the sack over her shoulder. She felt the weight of the promise she had made.

Roger's father was right. They had decided to take the Egg where it belonged. There was no sense in regrets now, and no thought of turning around. The only thing to do was to get the job done as quickly as possible.

They didn't talk much as they rode and as other travelers began to pass them by — a merchant with a loaded wagon; a farmer's wife with a cart full of onions to sell; a family on their way for an outing, the children in their cleanest clothes running ahead, the parents calling to them to wait. After a while Roger began to hum. Then to whistle. Then to sing under his breath to the rhythm of the horse's steady jogging pace.

"Kilian, kalian, damerson, dee,
Who made the dragons and set them free?
Heart of a serpent, voice of a man,
Breath of the fire that none can withstand."

"That's not how it goes," Mella objected, forgetting that she had planned to be polite.

"What?"

"The song. Those aren't the right words."

"Of course they are." Roger twisted to look over his shoulder, a little offended. "I've known that song since I was in the nursery. Everybody knows it."

Of course everybody knew it. Little children played a game with it, holding hands, spinning in a ring, faster and faster, until the end when they let go and everyone fell staggering and giggling to the ground. But Roger had gotten the words wrong. Mella chanted,

> *"Kilian, kalian, damerson, dee,*
> *Coel made the dragons and set them free.*
> *Skin of a serpent, mind of a man,*
> *Heart of a fire that none can withstand."*

"That's not right," Roger said when she'd finished.

"Of course it's right. Gran taught it to me."

"But it's—Coel *didn't* make the dragons. He fought them. Everybody knows that."

"It's just a game song," Mella answered. "It's not *history*. Like the nonsense words at the beginning. It's not supposed to mean anything." She pointed ahead. "Look, there's the ford."

There was no bridge over the river at Dragons-ford. The spring floods, when snow melted in the mountains, would sweep any such structure away.

Instead, at a shallow place, broad flat stones had been laid in the water so that horses and carts and humans could cross easily, wetting their feet but doing themselves no other harm.

The mare delicately picked her way across the river, and they were in the market town. All the old buildings in Dragonsford were stone built, with slate roofs, close to the river. But a ring of thatched, wooden buildings had sprung up around them.

Mella had known all her life that all the old buildings in the mountains were stone. It hadn't occurred to her to think why. Now, as the mare stepped onto the cobbled main street, she found herself thinking of the scorched trees and smoldering turf where Damien had fought the dragon.

How long had it been since a dragon had been seen near Dragonsford? Long enough for people to forget how fast a straw roof burned.

Over brown thatch and shingles of dark gray slate she could see the Dragontooth Mountains. Mella found she was holding her breath. The lower slopes were closely covered with dark green spruce, and above were hills of yellow green grass, and then mounds of bare gray rock that rose higher and higher, until her eye reached the peaks splashed white with snow.

Mella had seen those mountains every day of her life. But she hadn't quite realized until now just what she had promised to do. To carry the Egg into that wilderness?

Roger didn't seem troubled by the sight of the mountains like jagged teeth gnawing at the sky. "Do you know this town?" he asked her, raising his voice so she could hear him over the noise ahead.

"I've been here once," Mella answered. "For the market. Father always stays at the Red Hart when he comes." She pointed to the right.

Roger turned the mare off to the left. "Then we should stay elsewhere," he called. "In case they're looking for us."

He had to speak loudly because the main street of Dragonsford, running along the river, was thronged with loaded wagons, horses, oxen, donkeys, and people on foot. A shepherd urged his herd along, whistling at a black-eared dog who nipped flanks and nudged shoulders until the sheep turned the right way. Mella saw a tinker's caravan, red and green and yellow. A wagon passed by, loaded with dragons in cages; one of them hissed and beat its stubby wings. And over all the bleats and curses and shouts and laughter, the river itself hissed and churned among stones as it rushed down from the steep slopes of the mountains.

The inn they finally chose was far back from the river, a flimsy wooden structure that seemed to sag to one side. To Mella's mind, the innkeeper should have been ashamed of his dirty yard, his unpainted doorway, and the rank smell that wafted out from his stables. Her father would never have stood for such slovenliness. But surely no one would think to look for them here.

Beside them in the yard, a merchant had thrown back the cover over his wagon and was checking the goods inside. Mella glimpsed bolts of cloth, small barrels and chests, a case of small, dark bottles, before the man gave her an angry look and moved to block her view.

There was no evidence of other guests. Clearly this was not one of Dragonsford's more popular inns.

"I brought this," Mella said, and she pulled a bracelet over her wrist to show Roger. The chain was only brass, but there were three beads of red coral to match the five that hung from her necklace, tucked deep inside her sack for safekeeping. "It will pay for a night's lodging, don't you think?"

Roger shook his head.

Dismayed, Mella looked down at her treasured bit of jewelry. Da had taken it in trade from a merchant a year ago and given it, along with the necklace, to her. "But it's—"

"I meant, no, don't sell your bracelet. I have a little money. Enough for this."

Mella thought she should object. "It's my journey. The dragon laid it on me. I ought—"

"Save it in case we're in real need later," Roger said practically. "While I have coins, why not spend them?" He finished tying the mare to a hitching post, gave her a quick pat, and headed for the door of the inn. Mella slipped the chain back over her wrist and followed him.

When the innkeeper asked double what Mella's father would have charged for a room, she nearly objected. But Roger caught her eye and shook his head, warning her not to call attention to herself. So Mella just snorted in disapproval as Roger handed over five silver coins.

"And we'll need a fire in the room," Roger added. The innkeeper, his clothes and hair greasy and his fingernails edged with black, frowned.

"'Tis full spring. We only burn firewood in the winter."

"My sister's ill," Roger improvised. Mella took her cue and coughed, trying to look pale. "She needs the warmth." The man still looked unwilling, and Roger reached into his purse for another coin.

"Don't be such a skinflint, Han." The merchant

from the yard stood in the doorway, listening to the conversation. "Can't you see that these are not the quality of travelers you ordinarily entertain?"

The man's voice was mocking, but Mella could not tell who he was making fun of, herself or Roger or the innkeeper.

"If you take my advice," the man continued, eyeing the innkeeper hard, "you'll treat these two guests well indeed."

The innkeeper gave the merchant a puzzled, resentful look but muttered, "Well enough, well enough." Roger drew his hand back out of his purse.

The merchant gave Roger and Mella a friendly smile. He was handsome, with eyes of a keen blue and long fair hair braided smoothly down his back, and prosperous as well. A gold ring shone on his finger; his vest was fine green wool, dark to contrast with the long, narrow red silk scarf around his neck. Still, Mella found herself a little uneasy. She wanted to turn aside from his attention.

But the man had helped them, after all, and she

didn't want to act like a stupid peasant girl, frightened of everything in the city. And what was she afraid of? It was not as if they had anything to steal—the few coins in Roger's purse, her two bits of jewelry, and a dragon's egg. Hardly enough to tempt a rogue or a thief. She gave the man a nod of thanks before the innkeeper led them upstairs to their room.

The floor needed scrubbing, and the bedding could have used a good airing, Mella thought fastidiously. But at least the room had a fireplace and a door that shut and latched.

Mella took the metal box out of her sack and opened it to check on the Egg. It was still hot enough to redden the fingers she held nearly an inch above the black surface.

"You stay and wait for the fire," Roger said. "I'll go to the marketplace. We'll need food to travel into the mountains."

Mella nodded. She was having a hard time taking her eyes off the Egg. It was so dark it almost seemed to glow, she thought dreamily. It was like a hole in the air. She forgot to say farewell to Roger when he left. She forgot to argue that he should not spend his coins on what was, after all, her quest.

After a while she shut the box again, to keep the Egg's heat contained, and stowed it at the bottom of her sack. Yawning, she moved over to the bed and stretched out on top of the shabby quilt. She'd had less than a night's sleep, and this seemed like a good time to catch up. Her eyes had just drifted shut when she heard the door swing slowly open on its hinges. It must be the servant come to make up the fire. But she couldn't be troubled to open her eyes and make sure.

Chapter Eight

Mella had terrible dreams. She seemed to be drowning in black water; it pressed down on her face, keeping air from her lungs. She fought to swim, but her arms and legs wouldn't obey her. She could only float limply, helplessly, as she was tumbled over rapids and bumped against stones and at last dragged over the edge of a huge waterfall. The pool at the bottom was so deep that she never stopped going down.

It took a while for Mella to understand that she was awake. She was cold, as cold as if she truly were at the bottom of the deep black pool of her dreams, and she was lying on something rough and uncomfortable. What a terrible inn this was. The beds were hard as stone. She tried to reach up and rub her face, but something was wrong with her hands.

"Mella!"

Someone was calling her. It was Lilla's turn to light the fires. She should hurry. Then it wouldn't be so cold.

"Wake up. Mella, please. Wake up."

Lilla would never say please. Puzzled, Mella opened her eyes. It took her a few moments to realize that she was looking at her own hands, tied together at the wrists with fine, strong cord. Then fear burned away the last of her sleepy daze, and she sat bolt upright with a gasp.

She was sitting on the ground in a small clearing in the woods. It was a dark night, but the flickering, shifting orange light of a small fire let her see what was around her. Roger was not far away. His hands, like Mella's, had been bound together in front of him. Another rope was around his waist, tethering him to the back wheel of a wagon. Twisting around, Mella discovered that she was tied the same way. The rope was too short to allow her to turn and get at the knots unless she could free her hands.

"Thank goodness," Roger said, keeping his voice low. "I thought you were never going to wake up. I was getting worried."

"I'm *still* worried." Mella found her voice shaking. She tried to steady it. "What happened? I was in our room at that inn. . . ."

Roger shrugged. He was picking at the cord around his wrists with his teeth. "Someone grabbed me from behind in the marketplace. He put something over my face. It smelled terrible. When I woke up, I was in that wagon. You were there too."

"But who—"

Roger nodded at something across the clearing. Mella's question died in her throat.

A man walked out of the darkness between two trees, carrying an armful of firewood. He dropped the sticks to the ground and came over to crouch on his heels near Mella and Roger.

With his head tipped a bit to one side, he seemed to be looking them over as if they were dragons he was considering buying for his herd.

The firelight was at his back, casting his face in shadow. Mella could only get a glimpse of fair hair, smooth against his skull, and the glint of gold on one hand. The merchant, she thought. The one from the inn.

Suddenly, without speaking and without warning, the man reached forward and slapped Roger hard across the face. Mella gasped, but Roger didn't cry out, or even put up his bound hands to wipe away the trickle of blood that came from his nose.

"Leave those knots alone, or I'll tie your hands behind you," the man said pleasantly. "And you'll find that's a much less comfortable way to spend the night. Well, my little guests. I'm so pleased to see everyone awake. Did you have nice dreams?"

He chuckled when neither of them answered.

"We must not be strangers to each other. You

may call me Alain. It's as good a name as any. And you need not fear; I am no murderer. Indeed, I'll take very good care of you. Your father will pay handsomely, I'm sure, to have you back in one piece."

His eyes on Roger, he hardly seemed to notice that Mella was there. Somehow that made Mella angrier than being kidnapped and drugged and tied up.

Roger sat up very straight. His voice, when he spoke, was sharp. Mella stared at him. He didn't sound like friendly, inoffensive Roger anymore. He sounded like someone you wouldn't want to cross.

"And how long do you think *you'll* stay in one piece after my father has me back?"

Alain laughed again. "Why, as long as you want your little friend there to stay alive." He nodded at Mella, who felt her throat go cold and tight. "She'll make an excellent passport into the next kingdom, or even the next. It was very considerate of you to provide me with a hostage."

He reached out toward Roger's face again. Mella flinched, but the man only ruffled Roger's hair.

"Let's understand each other now. If you do as I say, I'll treat you well enough. But any trouble you cause me, you'll quickly regret. Meanwhile, let's see what gifts you brought me, shall we?" He got to his feet and walked around to the back of the wagon.

"Is your father rich?" Mella hissed at Roger.

"Very," Roger mumbled. He was chewing on the knots again.

"But how did that man know?"

Roger shrugged. "He must have—" He broke off and quickly lowered his hands as Alain came back around the corner of the wagon, carrying Mella's sack and the leather pack full of Roger's belongings.

Mella burned with helpless anger as the merchant emptied her sack, scattering its contents across the grass. "Let's see what we have here. I'd be a poor host to let my guests get cold, wouldn't I?" He tossed Mella's cloak at her. She wrapped it around her shoulders as best she could with her hands tied and watched while Alain picked up her coral necklace, dangled it from his fingers to examine it in the firelight, and flicked it aside into the grass. "Worthless. But what's this?" He picked up the metal box that held the Egg.

Mella exchanged a desperate glance with Roger as Alain flipped open the lid of the box. His eyebrows lifted.

"It's a firestone," Mella said quickly. "If you put it in the fire overnight, it will keep its heat all day."

"It's valuable," Roger added earnestly. "Worth . . . I don't know how much."

Still ignoring Mella, Alain looked at Roger with narrowed eyes. "I have never heard of a firestone."

"They're very rare," Roger told him. "It was a gift to my father. There are only five in the world. But you have to put it in the fire. If it grows cold, all its magic will be gone."

Alain studied Roger thoughtfully. Then he smiled.

"Put it in the fire, must I? And if I do, what then? It will burn to nothing? It will explode, perhaps?" He shut the lid of the box. "No, I'll take this to a business acquaintance of mine. I'm sure it must be important; you were so anxious to have me destroy it."

He dug through Roger's pack—an extra shirt, a dagger in its sheath, a small leather-bound book, a water-smoothed stone, an intricately curled shell. Something wrapped in a scrap of linen looked like it might be precious. Alain unwound it with interest only to find two birds' eggs, each a pale, unearthly blue, packed in dried moss to keep them safe. Alain snorted and crushed them between his thumb and finger. Roger, who hadn't made a sound when he was struck, winced.

Hefting Roger's purse in his hand, Alain frowned at its weight and poured its copper and silver coins into his hand. "Not much for your father's son," he said, sounding offended, as if Roger had cheated him in a bargain.

But Mella, even though surprised at Roger's wealth—she'd rarely seen so many coins together at one time—could not take her eyes off the box that held the Egg. It had not been in the fire since the night before. It would be getting cold, too cold.

She felt cold as well, with despair. Bad enough that they were in this man's power. But even if they could somehow manage to escape, it would be too late. The Egg would be dead.

Roger looked apologetically at Mella. *I tried*, his eyes said.

After dropping Roger's woolen cloak across the boy's lap, Alain went back to his wagon. With his own cloak and two blankets, he made himself a comfortable bed near the fire. He set the box with the Egg next to him, and beside it he laid a sword in its sheath, ready to his hand. "I sleep lightly," he warned them. "If you're wise, you'll try to get some sleep yourselves. We've a long journey tomorrow to a place where I can stow you safely before I begin my bargaining."

For a time, Mella thought she could see glints of light from his half-open eyes. But finally she dared to believe that he was actually asleep.

"What will we do?" she whispered at Roger.

"I don't know." He was back to working on the knots with his teeth. "He won't kill us, at any rate."

"But the Egg—it'll get cold!"

"I know."

"Well, then?"

"Well, what?"

"We have to—I don't know—we have to do *something*!"

"What, exactly, do you think we should do?" Roger asked patiently.

Mella found his calmness too exasperating to bear. "It's not *my* fault we're here," she hissed angrily.

"So it's mine?"

"*My* father's not the rich one! No one would hold *me* for ransom. And it's all very fine for you to say he won't kill us. You mean he won't kill *you*."

Roger didn't speak. Mella felt a little ashamed of her temper, until she realized that the reason Roger had not answered was because he was not listening. Instead, he was staring at something over her shoulder.

"What's—" He swallowed. "What's that?"

Mella turned to look.

Chapter Nine

Eyes. There were eyes in the tangled darkness between the trees, yellow spots of light a foot or so off the ground. They shifted and blinked and seemed to be creeping closer.

Dragons. Wild dragons.

One, bolder than the rest, was slinking quietly across the grass. Long neck stretched out, belly close to the ground, it crept toward the fire where Alain was sleeping.

"Is it going to . . . eat him?" Roger whispered, horrified.

"It's the Egg," Mella whispered back. "They want the Egg."

The dragon stopped. It sniffed around the box

holding the Egg and backed cautiously away from the fire, settling down in the grass with its nose toward the Egg.

Something brushed against Mella's side. She jumped, stifling a yelp that surely would have awakened Alain. A small brown dragon, a female, crept out from under the cart. It bared its fangs at Roger, who squirmed as far away as his bonds would allow.

"Hush," Mella breathed, hoping to soothe the creature. "Hush, all's well. . . ." Which it wasn't. More dragons were creeping in from the trees, closer to the fire and the Egg. If Alain slept as lightly as he claimed, any minute now the soft sighs and hissing, the rustle of clawed feet and long tails through grass and fallen leaves, might awaken him. And then? Mella couldn't imagine.

The little dragon beside Mella was quivering with urgency, her whole body pointing toward the Egg like a hunting dog on a scent. Without think-ing, Mella put her bound hands out to scratch behind the dragon's ears, exactly as she would have done to one of her own herd. And she thought of an idea.

She laid her fingers against the dragon's neck and tried to make her mind very quiet and still.

Help, she thought. *Help me.*

Nothing. Or did the dragon press a bit closer to Mella's side?

Help me, Mella urged.

Was she imagining it, or did she sense something of the dragon's mind? It wasn't as clear as a word or a thought. But there was a yearning, an excitement, a delight. The Egg was pulling the wild dragon like the moon pulled the tide.

I am the keeper, Mella thought. *Help me.*

The dragon's head swiveled around. Large yellow eyes, glowing dimly in the dark, studied Mella.

Mella held out her bound hands.

The dragon turned back to the Egg and crept off through the grass.

Mella could have cried. She'd been so sure. So sure the dragon would hear her, would help her.

But it had been foolish. A keeper could sense her own herd and know in her bones when her dragons were hungry or ill or frightened. But she could not do the same with another's herd. And these were wild dragons, not tame at all. Nothing in them was attuned to a keeper's mind.

The wild dragons—were there six? Ten? More? It was hard to tell in the fading firelight—settled down, their scaly skins changing color to blend perfectly with the dry grass and bare earth. Only the twitching of a tail from time to time betrayed their presence.

Roger was back to gnawing on the bonds around his wrists. "They *are* related," he muttered indistinctly at Mella. "If they . . . wan' the Egg . . . tha' much . . ."

"Could we talk about it later?" Mella hissed and began to chew on her own knots. But Roger had a considerable head start. Before she'd made any progress, he'd loosened the knots enough to seize the loops around his wrists with his teeth and drag them over his hands, taking a fair bit of skin along with them. He twisted around to get at the ropes holding him to the wagon wheel.

"Hurry," Mella whispered urgently, with a frantic look at Alain. He lay still as stone by the fire.

Roger spared her a quick look as he yanked at the knots behind him. *What do you think I'm doing?* it said clearly. Mella could have screamed with impatience. Finally the last knot yielded to his tugging, and he scrambled over to work on the cords around Mella's wrists.

A low laugh came from across the clearing. Roger froze and Mella's head snapped up to stare at Alain, who was sitting beside the fire. In no hurry, he reached out to seize a branch and stir the coals with it. The flames brightened, and in their light Mella saw Alain's teeth as he smiled.

"Very noble. You might have run off yourself, but you stay to help your friend. I expected no less of you."

Roger's gaze moved quickly from Alain to the edges of the clearing, back and forth, measuring distances.

"I'm quite a pleasant host, if my guests are obedient," Alain went on. "But now you've proven that you can't be trusted. A shame. Things will—"

"Sorry," Roger whispered to Mella and bolted for the woods.

Mella cried out, mostly from surprise. It was for the best, of course. If Roger escaped, he might be able to rescue Mella or get help. Obviously, it was better for one of them to be free than both captive.

That didn't stop her from feeling abandoned.

But Alain had been expecting such a move. He didn't even bother with his sword as he leaped up to chase after Roger, and he would have caught him easily, if he had not tripped over a dragon.

The creature rose with a startled squawk, beating its wings and hissing as Alain fell. Alain swore and looked back to see what had brought him down, but Roger looked back too. His hesitation let Alain, now on his hands and knees, lunge forward, get a hand on Roger's ankle, and send him headlong.

The dragon, a small brown female, made a dash

for the safety of the cart and huddled there, hidden behind the wheel Mella was still tied to. She puffed out clouds of steam, warm and damp against Mella's back. The other dragons didn't move, trusting to their stillness to keep them hidden.

As Mella watched helplessly, Roger thrashed, trying to kick Alain off. But he was no match for a full-grown man. In a moment Alain had him pinned to the ground, one hand on his shoulder, the other clamped around one wrist. With his free hand, Roger scrabbled up a handful of dirt and gravel and threw it in Alain's face.

Alain simply turned his head aside to shield his eyes and shifted his grasp from Roger's shoulder to his wrist. "Anyone would think you'd learned your fighting in the gutter," he said mildly. "Quite enough of this." Getting to his feet, he yanked Roger up as easily as if the boy were a doll stuffed with rags. With one hand twisted in the neck of Roger's tunic, pulling it tight enough to cut off his breath, Alain dragged his captive back toward the wagon. Choking, Roger stumbled after Alain, unable to do more than pull at his collar, trying desperately to loosen it.

Mella felt as if something were clamped around her own throat. *Stop it. You're hurting him!* She bit back her foolish words. Of course Alain was hurting Roger; that was the point. The dragon hidden behind her lashed her tail angrily as Alain came near. The tail spike pricked Mella's arm.

Alain threw Roger facedown in the dirt and knelt beside him, pinning the boy with a knee in the small of his back. Pulling the long silk scarf from around his neck, he used it to tie Roger's hands behind him.

He wasn't looking at Mella. Why should he? Roger was the prize, the one he wanted. The wild dragon under the cart had gone still, huddling close to the earth.

Mella twisted around as much as the rope holding her to the wagon wheel would allow. "Hush," she breathed. "Hush, stay still, hush now. . . ."

"I did warn you," Alain said. Roger, his face in

the dirt, made a muffled sound as his captor yanked the knot around his wrists tight. "If you'd done as you were told, we might all have been spared this unpleasantness."

Mella didn't know if the dragon understood her or not. Probably not. The creature stayed still out of instinct, hoping danger would pass her by unnoticed, and didn't stir even as Mella began to rub the cords around her wrists against the sharp tail spike.

One strand gave. Two. Three.

"You've no one to blame for this but yourself," Alain told Roger as he used the boy's own belt to tie his ankles together. "There. A night spent like that may teach you to obey your elders."

The last cord snapped. Mella's hands were free.

Roger, squirming to get his face up off the ground, lifted his chin and saw Mella twisting around to work on the ropes that held her to the wagon wheel.

"I'll make it next time," he said hoarsely, rolling over and struggling to sit up. "You're a fool to think this will work. Someone will come after me. And—and you—"

Keep talking! Mella thought, as if she could shout the words into Roger's mind. She tugged frantically at the rope. The cord was thin, the knots tight.

"Such defiance." Sitting back on his heels, studying Roger, Alain smiled. "Really, it's not quite what I expected."

"And you can't—you don't even know enough—" Roger was clearly running out of ideas. Alain frowned.

"You're stupid!" Roger burst out wildly. "A smuggler, I bet. A criminal. You'll never be able to—"

"Oh, for pity's sake. Another?"

Just as the knot gave way under Mella's fingers, Alain, with a sigh as though he were losing patience at last, got to his feet. In two long steps he was at the wagon, his hand around Mella's upper arm, lifting her clear off the ground.

"You've picked up some bad habits from your

friend," he said. "It seems you need a lesson in obedience as well."

Mella felt as if her arm would snap off at the shoulder. She kicked wildly. Alain laughed. The dragon hidden under the cart dashed out and sank her teeth into the back of Alain's knee.

With a yell, Alain let go of Mella's arm. The little dragon dodged out of the way as the two humans fell together, and Mella kicked and rolled her way free.

Alain rose to his hands and knees to find himself face-to-face with a wild dragon. She flapped her stubby wings frantically and hissed steam into Alain's eyes.

Mella scrambled to Roger's side and yanked at the belt around his feet.

Alain fell back, a hand to his face, and staggered up. Limping badly, he ran for his sword. All across the clearing dragons were rising from the grass like shadows coming to life. Hisses and growls echoed from every side.

Mella got Roger's feet free as Alain reached his

weapon. Dragons surrounded him now. He swung the blade, and they danced lightly and easily out of the way.

"Maybe you should run," Roger whispered as Mella tugged on the scarf around his wrists.

"No, I've almost—"

"Look—"

One dragon after another darted in toward Alain and then fell back. Alain was good with his sword, but it was like trying to fight mist. The little brown female crouched to avoid a swing of the blade, leaped up, and fastened her teeth in Alain's sword hand.

Alain howled in pain and dropped the weapon. The scarf around Roger's hands came loose and fell away.

"Come on!" Roger was up, pulling at Mella. But her feet foolishly stayed planted. "Mella!"

"The Egg!"

The dragons pressed in close around Alain's knees. One must have bitten him again, for he cursed, twisted, lost his balance, and fell.

That's how they hunt, Mella thought, horrified. A pack of wild dragons would worry and harass their prey until it fell. And then . . .

She remembered Alain hitting Roger, choking him. She remembered how lightly and easily he had threatened her own life.

But to stand and watch him eaten, bite by bite . . .

"Stop!" she shrieked.

Roger was running forward. He snatched up Alain's sword from the ground. And the dragons, after all, did not swarm forward to finish off the fallen man, but drew back.

Mella ran too. She looked around for a weapon and grabbed a gnarled piece of root from Alain's pile of firewood.

"Surrender!" Alain gasped, on his knees. His hands, one bloody, were spread out pleadingly. "I surrender, young knight."

Roger stood before him, both hands on the hilt of the sword, the tip just inches from Alain's throat. The weapon was heavy for him. The blade trembled a little and caught the firelight.

"It is against the rules of honor to strike an unarmed man," Alain said humbly. "I ask mercy."

Roger hesitated. His face, smeared with dirt, was doubtful.

Mella brought her piece of firewood down hard on the back of Alain's skull.

"I'm not a knight," she said, looking across Alain's crumpled body to Roger's astonished face. "I'm only an innkeeper's daughter. We don't have to worry so much about the rules of honor."

Chapter Ten

Before they tied the unconscious Alain to a wheel of his wagon, Roger found a bolt of clean white linen among his stores and carefully bandaged the man's bleeding hand and the bite behind his left knee, along with a second, shallower nip in the calf of that leg. Mella supposed this was something else concerned with the rules of honor.

They took turns sleeping and staying awake to keep an eye on Alain, who didn't stir, and on the Egg, glowing like a black jewel in the fire. The wild dragons lay in a circle, their noses toward the flames, their tails twitching. They hissed and showed their teeth if Roger came too near. But when it was Roger's turn to watch, Mella slept between two of them, as warm as if she were in her own bed.

When the morning light came, the dragons crept quietly toward the woods. Alain woke to find Mella and Roger rifling through the goods in his wagon, looking for breakfast. Mella had expected Roger to object, remembering how fussy he'd been over borrowing Damien's horse for a few days. "Isn't this stealing?" she asked pointedly as he carefully arranged a thick slice of cold bacon between two chunks of brown bread.

Roger looked honestly surprised. "Spoils of war," he said. "It's entirely different." He didn't seem to understand why Mella laughed.

After they'd eaten, Mella nodded toward Alain, still tugging at his bonds and grumbling blasphemously under his breath. "What are we going to do with him?"

Roger frowned, worried. "We can't leave him here to starve." In the morning light, Mella could see the bruise across his cheekbone where Alain had struck him. "But I can't . . . Mella, I can't just kill him. He's our prisoner. I can't hurt him."

Mella couldn't imagine Roger using a sword on a helpless, bound man. She couldn't imagine herself doing it either. It had been one thing to hit him last night. But this was different.

"Wait," Roger said suddenly. "I have an idea."

First they gathered their belongings and filled their sacks with Alain's food. The kidnapper had stopped cursing by now and slumped against the wagon wheel, sullen and silent.

"One more thing," Roger said with a slow smile. It made Mella think of the way he had sounded the night before when he'd warned Alain of his father's vengeance. He went to the back of the wagon.

Mella watched, puzzled at first, as Roger picked up bolts of cloth in his arms and carried them to the smoldering remains of the fire. He built the flames up again with fresh wood and began to toss armfuls of silk and brocade into the conflagration.

Alain groaned.

Mella joined in, breaking glass bottles against a rock and letting the dark, syrupy liquid inside run out. The sweet, heady smell made her blink.

"Spiced plum wine," Roger said with interest, coming over to look. "From the islands off Tyrene. I don't suppose you paid the taxes on it?"

Alain banged the back of his head against the wagon and looked sick with the pain.

After they had burned or broken or trampled everything Alain had in his stores, Roger knelt down behind the man and slightly loosened the ropes holding his hands.

"You should be able to work yourself free before noon," he said, coming around to look Alain in the face. The trader looked up at him without gratitude, rage tightening his jaw, as if Roger's mercy were more of an insult than malice would have been.

"If the wild dragons don't come back before then," Mella added spitefully. She supposed Roger was right that they couldn't leave Alain to starve. But that didn't mean she had to be nice to him. From the sudden pallor of his face, he didn't know that dragons never came out until sundown.

"And another thing," she added. "Dragon bites

always get infected." This part was true. She'd had enough nips from her own herd to know. "You'd better get that hand seen to by a healer. If you don't, by nightfall it'll be swollen to the size of a melon. So don't try to follow us. Because if we find you in the woods, out of your mind with fever, I won't let Roger help you."

Alain had camped by the side of a road that was not broad and well used like the highway from the Inn to Dragonsford. It was a dirt track, barely wide enough for a wagon. In one direction, it led back to Dragonsford. In the other, it twisted and wound its way among the foothills. To get farther into the mountains, they'd have to strike out through the woods.

"He could at least have taken us along a decent road," Roger grumbled, surveying the forest, thick with brambles and undergrowth. "We can't even take the horse through that. We'll have to go on foot."

"Very thoughtless of him," Mella agreed solemnly. Roger glanced at her and began to grin.

"Perhaps we should complain," he suggested.

Mella began to giggle so wildly she had to sit down on an old stump to catch her breath.

"I'm sorry," she said suddenly, looking up at Roger. He stood leaning with one hand against a tree trunk; with the other he tried, unsuccessfully, to rub the smile off his face. Mella had been wondering awkwardly all morning how she was going to apologize for her temper the night before. She was surprised to hear the words fall so easily off her tongue. "For what I said last night. That it was your fault."

"Well." Roger's smile was gone now, and he picked up the pack he had dropped and slung it over one shoulder. "You were right, I suppose. It was me he was after. You would have been safe and well if I hadn't been there."

Mella looked up at him in astonishment. He had already started to pick his way among the trees, and she had to snatch her sack and hurry to keep up. "That's nonsense!" she said sharply to Roger's back. "I've never heard anything so thick skulled in my life. You might as well say a man's to blame for getting robbed, since if he hadn't been there the thief wouldn't have been tempted."

Roger shrugged.

"Oh, well, then. Sulk if you please." Mella tossed her head the way Lilla did. "I was only trying to be civil."

Roger pointed wordlessly to something up ahead.

"What?"

"See that stream?" Only as wide across as Mella's outstretched arm, it tumbled across their path and plunged down a hillside. "The dragon said we're supposed to follow the river. That stream should lead us to it."

They made their way cautiously along the streambed, climbing over boulders, slipping on mud, ducking under low branches. At last the water fell over a final bank to spill into the river.

Mella grew to hate the river.

The footing along its bank seemed to alternate between rounded stones that slid under her weight and flats of sticky mud that swallowed her feet up to the ankles. Her skirts became so filthy that she tucked them up into her belt to shorten them—never mind what her mother would have said about letting Roger see her knees. She was sore and bruised from falling and from sleeping on the stony ground. And no matter how much she and Roger struggled, the mountains seemed to come no nearer.

On the second day of toiling upriver, they left the spruce forests behind. Trees became rare, except for the ragged line of them along the riverbank, and they saw no more wild dragons.

On the third day the food they had taken from Alain began to run low.

"We'll have to go on short rations," Roger said gloomily as they sat on a broad, flat stone to eat a midday meal.

Mella groaned dismally at the thought of walking painfully upstream on an empty stomach.

"There's nothing else for it. We could fish, I suppose." Roger looked doubtfully at the river, tumbling swiftly by, the water leaping and clawing its way over stones.

"Do you have hooks and line?" Mella inquired disagreeably.

"No," Roger admitted.

"Do you even know *how* to fish?" Mella had twisted her ankle on a loose rock. Somehow she felt that an argument with Roger would make it feel better.

"I thought you would know."

"Why should I?"

"Well, you're . . ." Roger looked lost. "From the country, I mean."

A peasant, he meant. "My father *buys* fish for the Inn when we need it," she said coldly, and shifted on the stone so that her back was to Roger, the rich man's son.

She heard him sigh and then get up. "I'm going to climb that rise there," he said.

Mella didn't ask why.

"To see if there's anything—berries or something. Or maybe an easier way north."

It was absolutely no use trying to pick a fight with Roger. He was so nice, it made Mella grind her teeth. If she hadn't seen him stand up to Alain, she wouldn't think he had any backbone at all.

The river flowed by, quick and cold, chalky white with rock dust washed down from the slopes of the mountain. Faintly, over the rush and roar of the swiftly moving water, Mella realized that she could hear something. Someone shouting.

Twisting around, Mella saw Roger on top of a small, stony outcrop that rose up over the river. He was jumping up and down, waving his arms. But he wasn't looking at Mella. He had his back to the river and to her. As she watched, he suddenly disappeared over the far edge of the rise and was gone from her sight.

What on earth? Limping a little on her sore ankle, Mella clambered up the slope after him. Had he gone mad? If he thought she was going to chase him all over the mountain . . .

When she got to the top of the outcrop and looked down, she thought at first glance that her fears had been true. Roger *had* gone mad. There he stood, in a valley below her, talking eagerly and gesturing to . . . nothing at all.

Then Mella blinked and saw more clearly. There *was* a man standing opposite Roger. She had not seen him at first because his sheepskin clothing, his weather-beaten skin, and his dull brown hair blended so perfectly into a background of tree trunks and dry leaves. And because he stood so still. He was like a tree himself, unmoving, as if rooted deep.

Roger saw Mella and waved at her to join them.

"A night's lodging?" Roger was saying as Mella arrived, having slid and scrambled her way down to them. "We can pay for beds and for food if you've any to spare."

Oh, yes! Mella could have cried with joy at the idea of sleeping dry and warm for one night, even if it was on nothing better than a blanket in front of a hearth. And *food*!

The man's face didn't change. Two dogs sat at his feet, one black with four white feet, the other white with a black splotch over one ear. They both cocked their heads, as if they were also giving thought to Roger's words. There was a long, considering pause before the shepherd spoke.

"And what are you doing here, two children, and all alone in the wilderness?"

"That's our business," Mella said. Roger jabbed her in the ribs with his elbow, but Mella could feel the weight of the Egg in her sack and she remembered the cold despair she had felt seeing it in Alain's hands. They couldn't reveal the purpose of their journey to every stranger they met.

"We're just travelers," Roger said, frowning at Mella. "But we can pay well for a bed tonight."

The man let several moments go by as he thought, and then he shook his head.

Mella couldn't believe it. "Why not?" she demanded. Couldn't the man see that they needed rest?

"I cannot take strangers in if I know so little of their errand. If you have an honest reason for wandering about the hills, you'd best tell it to me." His voice was like the roots of the trees, gnarled and knotted, somehow deep and dark brown and strong.

"*You're* wandering about the hills," Mella pointed out tartly. "Do you have an honest reason for it?"

Roger made a horrible face at her, but Mella saw a corner of the man's mouth twitch. "I am searching for a lamb. Eagle killed a ewe and took one of the babies back to its nest for the chicks."

"An emperor eagle?" Roger asked. Now it was Mella's turn to make a face at him. What on earth did it matter?

The man nodded.

"I saw one flying over a few minutes ago," Roger said, and pointed. "It had something in its claws, and it landed in a dead pine."

Mella was amazed. She had not noticed anything flying overhead, and even if she had, she would hardly have bothered to watch where it landed. But then, her mind had been mainly on her footing. Where had Roger found the time and the will to look up?

"Emperors don't usually kill their prey straight off," Roger went on. "They bring it back so the chicks can practice hunting. We might be able to get it if we hurry." And without waiting for an answer he started to scramble up the hill, leaving Mella and the shepherd and the dogs to follow.

Mella burned with exasperation as she climbed up the slope and slid down again to the riverbank. Why should they do this man a favor after he'd refused them a night's lodging? They didn't have time to clamber up and down trees, rescuing lambs for people who weren't even going to help them.

She didn't think it was anything to do with the rules of honor, or with being noble and a rich man's son. Other knights and their squires had stayed at the Inn from time to time, and they had been mostly noticeable for their arrogance. No, it was just Roger. Too nice by half. She would have to explain how you could spend too much time helping, Mella thought, forgetting how glad she'd been of Roger's helpfulness when she'd been scrubbing the floor at the Inn and frantic with worry about the Egg.

When Mella and the shepherd caught up with Roger, he was standing at the foot of a dead pine tree. A stiff gray skeleton, it rose high overhead. They could see the untidy clump of twigs that was the eagle's nest.

"It looks like the mother's gone," Roger said, stepping back and shading his eyes to look upward. "Out hunting again. If I hurry, I can climb up and get the lamb back."

The shepherd spoke. "Nay, you've no call, young one. 'Tis my flock."

"The tree won't hold you," Roger pointed out. The branches of the dead pine were dry and brittle, most broken off a foot or two from the trunk. In fact, Mella wasn't sure it would even hold Roger.

But before she could object or the shepherd could argue further, Roger had dropped his pack and was working his way up the lower branches. Mella stepped back to see him better. Close to the ground, the branches were near one another, and he made quick progress. But as he approached the nest, the branches grew thinner, with more space between them.

"If he falls . . ." she said angrily to the shepherd, but she had no words to finish the threat with. If Roger fell rescuing the stranger's lamb, what could she do? Nothing.

Just as now she could do nothing but watch.

The shepherd stood beside her, his head tipped back so that he could keep Roger in his sight. Mella felt as though she were climbing with Roger, the dry splintery bark flaking off under her fingers, her arm muscles pulling her weight up, her toes curling to hold onto the branches. When a branch snapped under Roger's weight and he swung for a moment by his hands, she felt her stomach lurch, as if her own feet were dangling over emptiness.

Carefully, Roger got his feet back onto a branch and moved slowly upward. He was higher now than the roof of the Inn. Another minute and he had reached the fork where the eagle had made her home.

Roger braced himself and leaned over the nest. Mella held her breath. He would need both hands to pick up the lamb. Faintly, Mella could hear the squawks of the frightened chicks. If the mother eagle was anywhere nearby, the sound would bring her rushing back. *Hurry,* Mella thought urgently at Roger.

But he didn't hurry, and she realized that he didn't dare. Slowly, Roger reached into the nest and then brought his hands back over the edge. He held something. Mella could not see it distinctly, but she knew it must be the lamb. Roger tucked the small shape inside his tunic and prepared to make his way back down.

The shepherd's black dog sat up and barked sharply. Mella gasped.

In the sky she saw a dark shape winging toward the tree. Toward the nest and Roger.

Chapter Eleven

Emperor eagles had wings wider than a man was tall. Their beaks could break bone. They could kill a sheep or a full-grown deer. Not even a hunting cat could scare an emperor eagle off a kill.

Mella shouted a warning just as the bird screamed a high-pitched, angry challenge to the intruder near its nest. Roger began to climb back down as fast as he could, clutching at branches, trying to keep the trunk of the tree between himself and the furious bird.

The eagle dove, but it was hampered by the spiky branches. Roger slipped, snatched at a branch, recovered. Mella's heart thumped against her ribs. He would fall. Even if the eagle didn't reach him, he would fall. He couldn't dodge an attacker, and hang on, *and* keep the lamb safe.

Mella grabbed up a stone and threw it with all her strength, but it fell far short of the eagle. The bird dove again, and Roger ducked his head between his arms to shield his face.

Mella heard a strange humming sound.

The shepherd had pulled a sling loose from his belt. It was simply a long strip of leather, wider in the middle than at the ends. He held the two loose ends in one hand and in the center of the strip, where the leather folded over on itself, he'd tucked a smooth, round river stone.

Now he swung the sling in a circle, making the humming sound Mella had heard. The leather strap moved so quickly that it looked as if the man had his hand in the center of a spinning wheel. With a flick of his wrist, the shepherd sent the stone flying at the eagle.

The missile crashed through dry twigs and must have struck home, for the eagle screamed in pain and rage and swooped away from the tree. The shepherd's second stone missed, but it kept the great bird at bay as Roger slithered and scrambled the rest of the way down the tree. Six feet from the ground he grasped a thick branch, swung for a moment, and then dropped to land in a heap on the pine needles at Mella's feet.

"Roger!" Mella bent over him. "Are you all right? You're bleeding!"

"I am?" The eagle's talons had raked a deep scratch across the back of Roger's neck and down his shoulder. Roger got up a little unsteadily and twisted around, trying to see the injury. Mella dabbed at the blood with her sleeve. "Ow, Mella, stop that, it hurts. I think the lamb's all right," Roger said, and reached into his tunic to pull out the little animal and hand it over.

The newborn creature looked tiny in the shepherd's large, brown fingers. It was so young that its wool was still damp, and it huddled into the man's hands and let out an occasional feeble, whimpering bleat.

Carefully, the shepherd wrapped the lamb in a scarf from his neck and tucked it inside his tunic, where the heat of his skin would keep it warm. Overhead, the eagle, perched now on her nest, screeched an angry warning, and Roger and Mella looked up nervously.

"Well, then," the shepherd said. "I suppose you'd best come home with me."

The shepherd's name, it turned out, was Gwyn. He and his family lived in a tiny village, five or six round houses, each with its barns and pens behind it, all neatly built from slabs of stone. The little settlement almost seemed to vanish into the landscape, so that you needed to be close by to see it at all.

Gwyn's wife, Lelan, was a small, plump, round-faced woman who fussed over the scratch on Roger's neck while her children watched, wide-eyed at the sight of strangers. Mella kept losing count—were there seven or eight? She could only be sure of Tobin, the oldest, a few years younger than she was, and of Jes, the baby he was holding, bouncing her gently to keep her quiet while his mother took care of Roger.

Lelan, Mella thought, talked more than enough to make up for her husband's silence.

"An eagle, you say? Aye, they're vicious creatures. And the damage they do to the flock at lambing, it's terrible. We try to keep the ewes in the pens when they're near to birthing, but there are always a few who get out to have their babies in the open. Sheep aren't the brainiest of creatures, that's the truth. But what was Gwyn thinking, sending a slip of a lad like you up a great tree to an eagle's nest?"

"He was too heavy," Roger explained, wincing as Lelan rubbed a greasy ointment into the cut. "Besides, he didn't really send—"

"You might have been killed, and surely a boy's life is worth more than a lamb's. I'll tell him so, have no fear. Now, off with that shirt, my dear, and I'll stitch up that tear in a half a moment."

Roger was halfway out of his shirt when Gwyn came in, ducking under the low lintel of the doorway, the dogs at his heels.

"Lamb'll do well enough," he said briefly. "Whose horse is that before Rhil's croft?"

"A stranger, indeed," Lelan answered. "Can you imagine, three strangers in one day! I can't remember it happening before. A gentleman, well spoken he is, and he says he's looking for someone. Supper in a moment, my dears. The oatcakes are just baking."

Another stranger? Here, in this tiny village? Mella met Roger's eyes with a feeling of unease, and he slowly pulled his shirt back on just as the door to Gwyn's croft swung open.

"Rhil," said Gwyn, in greeting and question all at once.

The man who stood in the doorway was gray haired and gray bearded, stocky, and frowning. Other villagers, behind him, peered over his shoulders.

"Gwyn," he said, with a nod. "I hear you've taken in two children for the night?"

"Right enough," Gwyn said as Lelan paused, a spoon poised above a pot of stew over the fire. Jes whined in Tobin's lap and held out her arms for her mother. "They did me a service."

"Someone is here who has an interest in them," Rhil said and stepped aside to let Alain into the room.

Mella felt a shriek leap up in her throat, but she strangled it before it had a chance to get out. Roger, too, jumped as if he'd been stung by a wasp. But there were people all around. Gwyn was standing close by. Alain could hardly kidnap them in front of an entire village.

"Yes, this is them," Alain said, shaking his head sorrowfully. He walked stiffly, as if it hurt him to put weight on his left knee. "Your mother's heartbroken," he told Mella reproachfully. "How could you worry her so?"

Words knotted up in Mella's mouth, and she

couldn't loosen one to get it out. Her mother? Well, her mother must be worried, true enough, she thought with a stab of guilt. But why should *Alain,* of all people—

"You know these children, master?" Gwyn asked.

"Know them? Aye, of course. This is my niece. My own sister's child."

All the knotted-up words burst out of Mella's mouth in a cry of outrage.

"That's not *true!*" she managed to say, gasping with indignation. "He's—he's a *thief,* he's a criminal, he's a *kidnapper—*"

But Alain was talking too, and Roger, and Rhil.

"Four days ago she ran away from home. She's always been a wild girl, but since she took up with this rogue here—"

"He's not Mella's uncle, we know him—"

"Master, now, the child says she doesn't know you."

"If it wasn't for my sister I'd not have bothered

to look for her at all. Nothing but trouble since the day she was born."

"It's a lie, he's lying!"

"And a thief as well, this time. Look in her sack. See if you don't find there the bracelet that's a match for this. She stole it from her own mother, the heartless thing that she is."

Mella choked as Alain held out his bandaged hand. Dangling from it was a necklace with five coral beads. When she'd last seen it, he had tossed it aside as worthless. With all that had happened that night, she'd completely forgotten to pick it up out of the grass.

"That's *mine*!" she said with fury. "He *stole* it from me!"

Frowning, Rhil picked up Mella's sack.

"That's mine!" Mella cried out again. But Gwyn's hand fell heavily on her shoulder.

"Hush a moment, child."

"But he—"

"You'll have your say. I warrant it."

Rhil's fingers looked thick and clumsy, but

they were surprisingly deft as he sorted through Mella's possessions and found the bracelet easily.

"There now," Alain said with satisfaction. "Didn't I say so?"

"Well enough." Rhil frowned at the trinket. "There's proof, of a sort."

"It's *not*!" Mella shouted.

"Let the child tell her side, Rhil." Gwyn's voice was sober, his hand firm on Mella's shoulder.

"Tell them, Mella." Roger nodded at her.

"He's not—" Mella caught her breath and tried to order her thoughts. "He's *not* my uncle. He stole that necklace from me. He's the thief!" Awkwardly, the story of their encounter with Alain came out, Roger nodding eagerly to confirm everything she said. There was silence in the little croft after she had finished.

"Dragons?" Rhil looked dubious. "Never heard of wild dragons attacking a man."

"Kidnapped you?" another villager, leaning in the doorway, asked. "Why, then?"

"Well, because . . . Roger's father . . . he's rich," Mella explained.

Alain laughed shortly. "Rich? *That* one?"

Roger—torn shirt, unwashed hair, dirty face, scratched hands—looked helplessly at Mella.

"You see?" Alain sighed. "What my sister's had to endure from this one, I can't tell you. Enough of this storytelling now. You're both to come home with me."

Roger, with two quick strides, crossed the room to stand by Mella's side.

"But it's not *true*!" Mella shouted.

"Why were you wandering the hills then?" Rhil asked fiercely, turning a sharp look on her. "Two children, alone in the mountains? If you weren't fleeing home for a good reason, what were you doing there?"

"We were . . ." Mella's voice faltered.

"We needed to—" Roger said at the same time.

"And what's this, then?" Rhil, still holding Mella's sack, was looking at something inside it. He reached in and drew out the metal box that held the Egg.

"Don't touch that!"

"Mella, don't—"

"What have you stolen this time, girl?"

"That's mine, that's *mine*—"

But the babble of voices hushed when Rhil flipped open the catch and lifted the lid.

"What *is* it?" Fascinated, Rhil tilted the box so that firelight flowed silkily across the glossy surface of the Egg.

"What have you stolen now, the pair of you?" Deftly, Alain lifted the box from Rhil's hands.

"Don't you touch that!"

Roger clutched at Mella's arm. "It's just a rock," he said sharply. "It's nothing valuable. Mella liked the color, that's all."

Alain shut the lid on the Egg smartly. "Enough of this. I must take these children home. Then they'll be no more trouble to you."

Rhil turned to Mella and Roger, his face serious. "Can you give me a better account of yourselves than you have so far?"

Roger looked steadily at Mella. Mella opened

her mouth and shut it again. What could she say that would be believed? She twisted to look up at Gwyn. "Please," she whispered. "Please, it's true—"

But Gwyn didn't look back at her. He was frowning at the metal box in Alain's hands. And when he spoke, his deep, low voice caught the attention of everyone in the tiny room.

"I don't believe that's yours to handle, master."

Hope flared up brightly in Mella's heart. Did the shepherd believe them after all?

Alain laughed shortly. "You can't mean you think it belongs to them? Two children?"

"You said she'd taken a bracelet. Not . . . such a thing as that."

Alain shrugged. "I told you she's a thief. Who knows where she took this from?"

"If it's not hers, it doesn't follow that it belongs to you."

Alain turned to Rhil. "This is idle talk. Surely you can see who's lying here?"

"Lies enough," Gwyn agreed before Rhil

could answer. "But because the children can't account well for themselves, that doesn't mean this man's words are true."

Alain snorted. "You've two stories to choose from. One of us must be telling the truth."

"Indeed?" Gwyn looked keenly at Alain. "Nothing so far as I can see shows that all three of you are not lying."

Chapter Twelve

The villagers shut Roger and Mella up in an empty croft while they talked over what to do with them. The small stone building had once been a stable, and it was windowless, with two small rooms but no door to connect them. Alain was in the other. They'd heard him arguing angrily and then shouting as the door had been shut on him and a heavy stone rolled in front of it to keep it closed. Then silence.

Lelan had insisted that the two children would not be left without food and warmth, so there was a small fire burning in a hearth against the wall, and they had warm oatcakes and fresh white cheese. But the food tasted flat and dull to Mella, and she felt cold down to her bones. She sat on the hearth while Roger, restless, walked around and around the room. After a while he stopped and came to crouch on his heels next to Mella.

"I'm sorry."

"What for?"

"Well, if I hadn't—I mean, if I had—"

"Killed him?"

Roger swallowed, his face pale in the firelight. He nodded.

"You couldn't have."

"I'm supposed to."

"Don't be stupid. I couldn't have either. It's not your fault."

If it was anybody's fault, it was hers. She was the keeper. She should have fought and kicked and bitten to get the Egg back in her hands, and then she should have run. She wouldn't cry now, as if she were no older than Jes. She wouldn't. But her hands felt light and empty and so cold. She'd never be warm again unless she could hold the Egg once more.

Mella pulled her knees up, wrapped her arms around them, and laid her head down. She lost track of how long she sat, listening to the whispery sound that the leather soles of Roger's boots made against the smooth dirt floor.

A new sound, someone breathing hard outside the door, made Mella raise her head. There came a grunt of effort and then a soft thud, like a heavy stone falling onto dirt.

She and Roger looked at each other, wide-eyed, and Mella rose to her feet as the door opened and Gwyn entered. In his hands was the box that held the Egg.

Mella burst forward, biting back a cry, her hands out. She would have fought him for the box, but he gave it to her easily and didn't speak a word, only stood closely watching as she knelt by the hearth, Roger at her shoulder. She opened up the box with shaking hands.

The Egg had not been in the fire since the night before. Had it been too long? Would it be too cold?

But the Egg was hot enough to send a cloud of

steam into the air when she released the catch and swung the box's lid open. In fact, it seemed warmer than Mella remembered it being, even just out of the fire. Could the Egg be getting hotter? And what would that mean? Could it be that it was getting closer to hatching?

No time to worry about that now. Thank goodness her gloves were in her pocket and not in the sack that Rhil had taken from her. She slid them on and picked up the Egg, settling it carefully into the heart of their small fire, and piled coals around it until it was almost covered.

Gwyn had observed all this in silence. Now he came to crouch beside the fire, his eyes on the Egg glowing black in a nest of coals.

"Now," he said. "Tell me how you came by this. And what you mean to do with it."

Roger glanced at Mella doubtfully. She was as unsure as he was. Gwyn had brought the Egg back to them — but why? Should they tell him the truth? What would happen if they did?

But they could hardly be worse off than they

were now. Lying and silence had done them no favors and earned them no help.

Gwyn didn't press them but waited quietly for them to decide. In the orange gold light of the fire, something gleamed white at the collar of his tunic. A slender piece of ivory, slightly curved and longer than a man's finger, hung from a leather cord around his neck.

They had to try trusting him, Mella thought.

The cave. The Egg. The dying dragon and the promise. Stumbling, backtracking, with occasional additions from Roger, Mella told the story.

"Follow the river to a waterfall," Gwyn said thoughtfully when she had finished. "That's where you're headed?"

Mella and Roger both nodded.

"Then be ready." Gwyn got to his feet, giving the Egg one last look. "Before dawn, I'll be back to take you there."

On Roger's advice, Mella slept away as much of the night as she could. Gwyn had said that it was moonless, too dark and too dangerous to wander about the mountainside; he would come back for them when dawn was nearer. She hoped he was telling the truth. But at any rate, the Egg must stay in the fire as long as possible. There was no point in going on if it got too cold to survive.

It was still black as the inside of a chimney when Gwyn heaved the stone away from the door a second time and called them softly from the doorway. Hurrying, Mella plucked the Egg from the fire. She could feel the bite of its heat even through her gloves as she packed it away in the metal box.

The stars were hidden behind clouds. Mella clutched the box tightly under one arm and with her free hand clung to Roger, fearing that if she let go, the greedy blackness would swallow him up. Roger, in turn, held onto Gwyn as he led them quickly around the backs of small houses and sheep pens and out into the stony mountain slopes that surrounded the village.

No one attempted to speak. At first Mella was

afraid of being overheard, and later she was too busy trying to keep her footing. When they were well away from the village, Gwyn lit a small lantern, which made it easier to follow him. But it did little to help Mella see where she was walking. The ground under her feet was crafty, plotting against her. No two steps were the same. She staggered in hollows, tripped over roots and hummocks, slipped on unsteady stones. More than once Roger's hand kept her from falling.

The night took away all her sense of time as well. Gywn had said he'd come for them before dawn—but how much before? She couldn't tell. Sounds were odd in the darkness as well. Her own breathing was too loud, almost as if it were coming from somewhere behind her. And some-times there seemed to be a noise following her—a rustling or muffled thumps like someone walking on packed earth. But it stopped whenever they did, so it must be nothing more than the echo of her own footsteps. Mella put the thought of hunting cats firmly out of her mind and kept going.

After a while—more than minutes, less than hours—she noticed something: not light returning, but the darkness lessening. The path Gwyn followed showed itself as a wavering strip slightly darker than the grass surrounding it. If she looked hard at the ground, she could see holes before she stepped in them. Roger's hand, light against his dark sleeve, was dimly visible.

Even so, when Roger stopped she nearly walked into him. "What is it?" she hissed.

"I don't know. He said to wait."

The glow of the lantern had moved off to their left. Then Gwyn's voice came out of the darkness.

"Come, you two. It's not long until dawn, but we can rest safely here a while."

"What is this place?" Roger asked as they huddled together. Gwyn had found a little stone shelter with only three walls, barely big enough for the three of them, and so low that the shepherd could not have stood up inside. But it did help to keep them from the worst chill of the night air.

Gwyn shrugged. "Built long ago, it was. If a man's caught out on the mountain overnight, looking for his sheep, he'll shelter here."

Mella looked up at him, and his weathered face, half revealed and half concealed in the dim lantern light.

"Tell us why," she said. "Why are you helping us?"

Gwyn touched the pendant around his neck.

"It was laid on me." His voice was rough and low, and his gaze stayed on the metal box in Mella's hands. "On all the oldest sons of my family, back further than I know. To help if we could. My father told me there had been a great betrayal, and only a few were left to set it right."

"Betrayal?" Roger's interest was caught. "Who betrayed someone? When?"

"I do not know. Nor did he. Long ago, he said. Here, now." From a sack he carried, he took out two thick cloaks lined with sheepskin and handed one to each of the children. Mella wrapped hers around her shoulders, grateful for the soft warmth. "Lelan would not rest, thinking you might be cold in the night." He took out a water skin, too, and dry oakcakes, now broken into pieces by their journey. "'They're only children,' she told me. 'Mind you look after them.'"

"And so I will. I promise you." Alain stepped out of the darkness, into the dim circle of light cast by the lantern, his sword out and pointed toward them.

Mella sat upright, frozen, clutching the box holding the Egg to her chest. Roger grabbed at an oatcake as if it were a weapon. Gwyn didn't move.

Alain smiled cheerfully.

"A dragon's egg? And you believed that? They told me it was a magic firestone. But I've the sense to know a lie when I hear it." He'd been listening, Mella realized with horror. They'd told Gwyn their story in that tiny croft, with Alain on the other side of a wall. How could they have been so careless? And how had Alain gotten out? Had he shoved his door open against the weight of the stone keeping it closed, dug out through the earthen floor, loosened a rock in the wall? Did it matter?

"But I have to thank you for your willingness to believe in fairy tales," Alain went on. "And for bringing the children out here, where there'd be no one to help them."

Mella wanted to burst into tears. It simply wasn't *fair* to have their last chance snatched away like this. They'd escaped, she had the Egg in her hands once more, and now . . .

On the floor of the tiny shelter, along one wall, there lay a long wooden staff. Some shepherd, who knew how long ago, had sheltered here and forgotten his crook. Gwyn reached out a hand and picked it up as he got to his feet, stepping out of the shelter to stand between Alain and the children. Alain laughed.

"A staff against a sword? A fool's game."

Smoothly Gwyn reached behind him, using the tip of the staff to knock the lantern over. Its light flared and vanished as it hit the ground.

"Run," he said calmly, a voice in the darkness.

Mella scrambled out of the shelter on her knees and one hand, hugging the box to her with the other. Roger ran into her as she gained her feet, and the two of them stumbled and staggered away from Gwyn and Alain. Behind them Mella heard thumps and grunts and then a sharp cry.

The darkness around them was no longer absolute. Rocks and holes in the ground were black splotches in the sparse mountain grass. Not far away, across a stretch of that pale gray grass, a line of darkness rose against the sky. Trees, Mella hoped. Something to hide them. She ran in that direction, plowed through a thin curtain of under-brush, and dove under the shadows of tall spruces and pines. The faint predawn light could do little to lift the darkness under there. Tree trunks loomed up suddenly from one side, then the other. She dodged around them and felt the ground under her feet suddenly give way. From behind, Roger ran full tilt into her.

She was rolling, tumbling, hugging the Egg close to her and unable to use her arms to break her fall. Roger's knee smacked into the side of her head. Together they skidded and slid down a slope and landed with a thump on a stony scrap of beach, next to a river that ran quick and cold and deep through a ravine.

Mella caught her breath, shook her head clear, and staggered to her feet. She still had the box, and inside it, the Egg. That was what mattered, not her bruises or her scrapes or her throbbing head. "Hurry," she told Roger. "Come on—"

But Roger shook his head.

"What?" Mella wanted to whisper, but the river, rushing swiftly by, was too loud to let a whisper be heard. Her eyes were adjusting now to the faint light, or the lack of it. She could see Roger's face, twisted as if he were in pain, looking up the slope they had just fallen down and then back at her.

"I can't, Mella."

"You can't *what*?" How could he just stand there? Any moment now Alain might appear on the top of the slope, laughing down at them.

"I can't just leave him!"

Shame flooded Mella, hot and bitter. Gwyn. Alain had a sword and knew how to use it. Gwyn was a shepherd with nothing more than a wooden stick. And they'd run off and left him to a fight he could not win.

"Alain will kill him. I have to—"

"But—" Mella hugged the box to her. "But—"

"You go on." Roger gestured upstream. "Stay down by the river. You won't be seen. I hope. If I—I'll come if—you keep the Egg safe. Go on. Go!"

Roger turned and began scrambling on hands and knees up the side of the ravine. Gravel and dirt kicked loose by his feet rained down around Mella. As she watched, he flung himself over the edge and was gone.

Mella stood there by the river, feeling as if she'd soon be torn in two.

She had to keep the Egg safe.

She had to help Roger.

She'd promised the dragon.

Roger was her friend.

But she was a keeper. The Egg was hers to watch over. Her hands tightened around the metal box until its corners bit into her palms. She had to—she had to—

With a groan, Mella turned and began running upstream along the riverbank.

Chapter Thirteen

She must *hide* the Egg. That's what she would do. She'd find a spot under the roots of a tree or between two stones, somewhere sheltered and dark. Then she'd run back to help Roger.

And if Alain had captured Roger? And seized hold of her too? Then what would happen to the Egg?

And Alain surely would do so. Roger was only a boy. He didn't even have his dagger anymore; that had been taken from them when the villagers had locked them up. A boy and a shepherd against a ruthless armed man. Roger had been a fool to go back. A fool . . . but a brave one. It must be something to do with the rules of honor again.

Mella began to think that she might come to hate the rules of honor.

Somewhere above the walls of the ravine, the sun was rising. Mella could not see it, but she could see—almost feel—the darkness around her lightening. The sky overhead had begun to fade from black to a deep, cold blue. Mella could at least see her way along the thin strip of beach as she ran, stones tilting and shifting underfoot. She scrambled and tripped over branches scattered across the dry land when the river was in flood.

The farther she went, the deeper the river grew, and the louder it rushed through its bed. The noise it made would hide the sound of any pursuit, Mella thought. She'd never hear Alain until he was upon her. She risked a glance back, but a rock tilted under her foot, nearly throwing her to the ground. If she twisted an ankle now, she'd never save the Egg. Clearly she could not afford to look behind her. All she could do was run.

The sound of water against stone seemed to numb the thoughts in Mella's brain. The wordless roar poured over her, leaving room for only one idea in her mind, and even that was less an idea than an urge, a spur to her feet and her faltering breath. *Hurry. Keep the Egg safe. You're a keeper. Watch over it. Hurry.*

The ravine was narrowing. Soon the little strip of beach would cease to exist entirely, and Mella would be forced to wade in the river or climb the ravine's walls. She dipped a hand experimentally in the icy water and drew it back with a shudder as she felt the tug of the current. She could not wade in that. It would pull her down at the first misstep.

Up, then. Hugging the box under one arm, she began to climb the ravine wall. She could have done it easily if she had not been holding something; the dirt was soft and there were exposed roots to cling to. But the box hampered her, slowed her progress, and once nearly slipped out of her grasp entirely. She had to stop, digging in her toes and one elbow, and clutch the box with both hands. Her heart pounded as she pictured the box with the Egg inside bouncing down the ravine wall to splash in the river and be swept away.

No time to rest and pant and get over the fright. She must keep going. Looking up, Mella discovered that she was closer to the top than she'd realized. She balanced the box on a root, kicked and clawed her way up over the edge of the ravine, and then reached down to seize the box and bring it with her.

Sound hammered at her, loud as a herd of horses shod with iron clattering over a paved roadway. For the first time, Mella realized where Gwyn had been taking them.

Not far away, an entire river came roaring down a cliff face, straight as an arrow. The water did not simply fall; it plunged over the cliff as if eager to reach the ground and dove with a deafening crash into a deep pool. No, to call it a pool was wrong, Mella thought, as she reached its edge. A pool was something quiet and calm. This was a cauldron. It seethed and boiled madly, churning up a froth of white bubbles in black water. It seemed as though the water fought to escape from its stone prison, writhing and struggling until it leaped through a gap between two boulders and spilled down to another, quieter pool a few feet below. From there it swirled away down the ravine she had just climbed.

Thoughts of Roger and Alain and Gwyn drained out of Mella's mind. Clutching the Egg, she stood staring at the cliffs rising far overhead.

Follow the river to a waterfall, the dragon had said. It had not, apparently, given any thought to what she would do when she *reached* the waterfall.

Oh, it was easy enough for a creature with wings. It had flown lightly over those cliffs, following the bright line of the river below. Had it even thought, when it gave the Egg to her, of how an earthbound creature would make its way up the cliff? Had it realized what it was asking her to do?

Could a dragon understand what it meant not to be able to fly?

It was hopeless. Mella stood at the edge of the pool, the spray from the waterfall chilly against her face. It wasn't fair, it wasn't right, for them to have come so far and tried so hard only to come up against a wall of stone.

She stood there thinking this until she fell in.

The fine mist that drifted up from the falling water had softened the earth where Mella stood, loosening its hold on the rock beneath. It only shifted a little under her weight, but that was enough.

She did not feel herself falling. One minute she stood on the bank; the next she was in water so cold that the shock of it cut off her breath. The current grabbed at her with greedy fingers. She was pulled and dragged and tossed until she could not tell which way she should try to swim.

Her head broke above the water and she snatched in a quick breath before being yanked down again. The water tossed her up and slammed her against a boulder, held her pinned there. She clung with both hands to the slippery rock and coughed and breathed. But she could not hold on. The water tugged at her persistently until her cold, stiff fingers slipped, and then she was falling.

Mella didn't realize at first that the current had pulled her through the gap between two boulders down to the next pool. She only knew that she was tumbling through the air, and then that she was pushed, pounded, held deep under by the force of the water above her. The ache in her lungs spread to her entire body. She went down, down, and there was nothing she could touch but that angry water. Nothing to help her fight against it.

There! Her feet slammed against rock. She pushed herself off as hard as she could. Now the water seemed to be helping her, lifting her up, and she got a breath only to be pulled back down. The weight of the heavy cloak around her shoulders was strangling her, and she clawed at the strings around her throat with numb fingers, finally snapping them free.

The cloak dropped loose and the water swept her up. She breathed again. And this time the water did not snatch her back. It seemed to have tired of her and spit her out to roll, helpless, among the rocks until she fetched up against a wide, flat stone. She held on to it and blinked water out of her eyes until she could see again. She was near the shore, and next to the stone she held on to there was another, and another, rectangular blocks that almost looked as if they had been cut and shaped.

She pulled herself along the helpful rocks until she could crawl onto dry land, hardly able to breathe for coughing. She would choke, Mella thought, she hadn't drowned but she'd die here on the bank, unable to get air into her lungs. But slowly the spasms eased, and she was able to snatch in half breaths of air between fits. Finally she spat out a mouthful of muddy water and sat up. Her arms wrapped around her knees for warmth, and her wet, cold hands clutched at each other.

Each hand held the other.

She wasn't holding the Egg.

Her head jerked up, her eyes searching the churning water of the pool. But it was useless. Even if she could somehow glimpse the box that held the Egg in that torrent of black water and white foam, even if she could fish it out without drowning, even if it hadn't been battered to pieces—the water was icy. Far too cold for the Egg to endure.

She'd lost the Egg. It was gone.

That water—it had been savage, pulling at her, dragging her down. If she'd held on to the box, she'd never have been able to swim.

No excuses, girl. That was Gran's voice in her ear. *Do you think you can explain to dragons? All beasts know is that you're there or you're not. Excuses are nothing a dragon can understand.*

I tried, Gran, Mella whispered in her mind. *I tried. As hard as I could.*

But there was no answer. And Mella knew it

didn't matter. It didn't matter how hard she'd tried to save the Egg. It didn't matter how hard she'd tried to save Lady.

Lady had been Gran's favorite dragon. Mella's too, with her warm yellow scales so bright they were almost golden, her brown eyes, her elegant dignity. All the other dragons gave way for her.

After Gran died Lady wouldn't eat. Wouldn't raise her head up off her nest. All of Mella's coaxing, the kitchen scraps she'd begged from Mama, the hours she spent curled up by Lady's nest, scratching her ears, talking to her—it had been worthless. In her first month as a keeper, Mella hadn't been able to keep the queen of her herd from dying.

Take care of them, girl. Watch over them. But she hadn't been able to. And now she'd left them. Left her herd alone and traipsed off into the mountains to save a dragon's egg. And she'd failed in that too.

Not much of a keeper, Mella thought miserably, hardly aware of the tears on her wet cheeks. Nothing like Gran.

How nice it would be just to melt in her misery. To drain away among the stones and never have to get up again. Never try to do something she could not accomplish. Like taking a dragon's egg to its hatching ground. Or becoming a keeper at the age of twelve.

But there was Gran's voice again. *Tears mend nothing.*

"I know, Gran," Mella whispered. "Work mends all."

But what did you do when there was no work left to be done? When you had tried as hard as you could and had failed? What did you do when you had lost an Egg or let a dragon die?

You found something else to work at, that's what you did.

She may have been little use as a keeper, but that did not mean she had to fail as a friend. Roger needed her. She'd have to get up, make her way downstream, creep unseen through trees and brush, and figure out how best to help Roger.

So Mella lifted her head from her knees and

looked around her. The first step toward helping Roger was figuring out how to cross back to the other side of the river.

She was huddled on a narrow crescent of stony beach beside the pool. To her left, close enough that she could touch it, a wall of rock rose up just higher than her head. She had fallen down that height when the current had pulled her to this second pool. But it would do her no good to climb back up to the level of the water-fall. She could hardly plunge back into that pool again and expect to survive.

No, she'd have to make her way down the ravine—if she could. To her right, the water poured away down the gully, fast and powerful. Thank goodness the current had not pulled her down *that,* Mella thought, or she'd have drowned for sure. If she hadn't fetched up against those rocks . . .

Something else had been saved by the rocks as well. Her cloak, the one Gwyn had given her, was clinging to the side of a flat stone block. Mella got up and went to retrieve it, wading in cautiously up to her ankles and leaning over to snatch at it.

The edges of the rock that had snagged the cloak were rounded now by water and time, but once it had been square. Mella frowned. She shouldn't be wasting time, she must hurry to help Roger, but now her attention was caught and she couldn't help looking. Running water had never shaped a stone like this, with such flat sides and smooth, straight edges. Across the pool, on the opposite side, she could glimpse a few similar rocks, half buried in mud and gravel at the water's edge. For an instant her imagination sketched in what must have lain between them: a bridge arching across the tumultuous water below.

A bridge? Here? Why would anybody build it? This was wilderness. On one side of the river were trees and rocks and stony plains; on the other side would be more of the same. Who would want to get from one side to the other badly enough to build a bridge?

And there, in the trees on the other side of the water, what was that? Something moving. Somebody running and shouting. Which was silly. As if anybody could hear a word over the noise of the waterfall.

Roger waved wildly at her and then ran off downstream, quickly lost to Mella's sight among the trees. Mella, her wits numbed by cold and exhaustion, stared after him blankly for a moment before she understood. There might be a safer place to cross down below. If he could find it, he would come back to her.

Well. It seemed that she didn't need to go and save Roger after all. Which was good, because her knees were shaking with cold. She wrung water out of her cloak as best she could and wrapped it around herself. Even wet, wool and fleece would be better than nothing.

It wasn't long before Roger burst through the undergrowth downstream and ran up to her, soaked to the waist. "Are you all right?" he gasped. He nearly had to yell for her to hear him over the roaring water. "You're wet. You're *freezing*. Did you fall in? Mella? Are you hurt? Can't you answer me?"

"I lost it," Mella said with difficulty between her chattering teeth.

"What?"

"I dropped it. It's gone." She gestured vaguely at the waterfall and the seething pool.

Roger, shaking his head, was saying something she couldn't hear. He was pushing something into her cold hands. Something heavy and warm with flat sides and sharp corners.

"I found it by the other edge of the pool," Roger said. "You must have dropped it when you fell in. You fell in, didn't you? How did you ever get out? Mella? Don't cry. Are you all right? We can't just sit here. Come on." He tugged her to her feet. "We've got to find somewhere safe. We've got to hide."

Mella was better than all right—she was dazed, stunned, dizzy with relief. The Egg. She hadn't lost it. She hadn't destroyed it. It was still hers to watch over. The heat of the box in her hands was banishing the cold that had gripped her, and joy was warming her from the inside out. She could have flung her arms around Roger. She could have kissed him. But he was pulling at her, urging her away into the trees, and she remembered why he'd left her in the first place.

"Alain! What—"

"No, not Alain. He's . . . well . . ."

"He's what?"

Roger shrugged, looking almost embarrassed. "I—um. Hit him. With a rock."

"You did?" Roger nodded.

"What about Gwyn? Is he—"

"Later. I'll tell you later. Come *on*, Mella. We have to get away from here." He was tugging her downstream, toward the ravine.

"We—what?" Mella clutched the Egg close, almost as if Roger had made a move to take it from her. "Leave? You want to leave?"

"Well—what else?"

"We *can't* leave." Her anger was as warming

as the Egg, and she pulled away from Roger. "We've been trying to get here for days! We're closer than ever!"

"Mella, look. It's a cliff!" Roger gestured at the waterfall, the wall of rock. "We can't climb it. What do you want us to do?"

"I won't leave!" Mella heard her voice in her own ears. She sounded much younger than she was. She wouldn't cry; she wouldn't do it. Furiously she turned her back on Roger and, simply because he wanted to go downstream, she began scrambling up. A series of flat stones, almost like steps, brought her up to the level of the first pool. "You do what you want," she flung back over her shoulder at Roger, who followed her, protesting. "The Egg's mine. I have to take care of it. You can slink off downstream like a — like a —" She couldn't find a word to finish the insult, but Roger very likely couldn't hear her anyway.

As usual, it was hopeless trying to pick a fight with Roger. When they stood again at the level of the first pool, at the foot of the thundering waterfall, he touched her shoulder very lightly and gently. "Mella." He had to get his mouth very close to her ear to speak so quietly and still be heard over the din of the water. "We'll find another way. But there's nothing to help us here."

Mella pointed a trembling finger.

"There's that," she said.

Chapter Fourteen

What Mella had noticed was a crack in the cliff face. A thin black gap in the stone ran from the height of her shoulder to her knee. It was something she never would have seen from the other side of the river.

But now that she was standing before it, she could see that it was too narrow to let her climb through. Frustrated, she grabbed at the stones, leaning forward and trying to peer into the sooty blackness. Something shifted under her hands.

"Mella, look at this."

Mella pushed. A chunk of stone gave way and fell, clattering into the darkness inside.

"We can get in. We can, if we try. Roger—"

"Mella, *look*."

Roger's hand seized her shoulder and pulled her back. Mella boiled with impatience. What was he *doing*? That crack in the cliff seemed to tug at her. Perhaps it led nowhere. Perhaps it was only a few yards deep. But it was a chance, a chance that the dragon had not given them hopeless directions after all, a chance that they did not have to creep away defeated to hide in the woods, carrying the Egg with them.

And now Roger wanted her to *look*? At what?

"Don't you see?"

And Mella did see.

There was a faint outline in the rock, the shape of an arch. Her crack was along one edge. Mella had seen things like this before, in old stone buildings that had changed over time, where someone had blocked up a window or walled up a door. You could never hide the original opening completely.

She wasn't looking at the mouth of a natural cave. She was looking at a door, filled up with stone and mortar long ago. Long enough for mortar to dry and crack, for stones to fall.

A door in a mountain? Why?

Then Roger's hand swung her around, forcing her to look across the pool. At first she didn't see what he was pointing at. Through a stand of trees across a bare, stony plain, she caught a glimpse of movement. People, many of them. Light flashed on something as shiny as polished metal. Something red and yellow flapped like a curtain in the wind.

Mella darted forward again, pushing at the rocks. She shoved one inside, and more fell with it, tumbling into the darkness. The crack was almost big enough now for her to squeeze through.

Roger was at her shoulder, clutching branches and a handful of dried moss for tinder. He pushed frantically at another big block of stone in the cliff face, loosening it until it fell inward with a crash. They scrambled through the gap they had made. "Here." Roger, beside Mella, scrabbled at his feet for the fallen rocks. "Hurry."

Together, they pushed heavy blocks of stones

back into place in the wall behind them, blocking up the hole. "Who are those people?" Mella gasped as she shoved one into place.

"Does it . . . matter?" Roger panted, balancing a stone on top of hers. "Here—the last one—help me—"

They pushed the final block of stone into place above their heads. Mella expected thick darkness to close around them as they did so. But there was still light from somewhere, faint but enough to reveal rough stone walls and an arched ceiling overhead. They were in a tunnel, perhaps fifteen feet long, and the light came from the other end.

As Mella reached the end of the tunnel and peered out, empty space seemed to swoop in from either side. It took her a moment to realize that the dim, shadowless light came through holes in the wall above the tunnel's opening, holes that must be connected to shafts leading to the cliff face.

The room before her was far bigger than the common room of the Inn, and the ceiling drifted off into emptiness. Dust lay inches thick on the floor. There had been long tables in the center of the room; most were broken now, their legs disintegrated, their tops canted awkwardly on the floor. One still stood; on it was a tangled contraption of rusted metal and broken glass. Along one wall, a set of tall shelves had rotted and broken, and their contents had slid to the floor, a jumbled heap of shattered pottery, shards of glass, odd pieces of metal — that might have been a knife, that perhaps a many-armed candlestick — all hidden beneath a coating of dust and cobwebs like ghostly, gray white fur.

"What *is* this place?" Roger breathed, turning slowly around.

Mella couldn't answer him. Along the wall to her left, there were what looked like a row of small pens, closed in by waist-high stone walls. She'd seen walls just like that behind Gwyn's home. Walls for holding animals like sheep . . . or dragons.

Leaving Roger wandering off in the other direction, Mella came to lean against one of the low stone walls and peer into the pen. In one corner was a heap of stones and gravel. And on top of that was a pile of old bones.

Mella's feet crunched on something hard but fragile. She knelt to run her hands beneath the dust and found herself holding dragon scales.

Her stomach quivered as she stared at the bones on the stone nest. Had whoever walled up that doorway left dragons in here to die? What keeper would have left dragons behind?

"Someone was raising dragons here," she said to Roger.

No one answered her.

Turning back, she glimpsed Roger across the room from her, studying something in the far wall. She walked toward him, past the arched doorway to the tunnel, past a fireplace so big she could have stood up easily inside it, ashes still heaped in its corners. Her feet scuffed through the dust on the hearth, and she sneezed and looked down, blinking to clear her eyes. The stone floor was scorched and blackened, as if the fire had raged out of control. With her toe, she nudged something beneath the dust—a heavy iron ring, attached to a rusted chain driven into the wall.

For no reason she could name, a shudder rippled along the skin of her scalp and neck.

"Dragons," she told Roger as she came up behind him. "I think someone was breeding dragons here."

"I think so, too. Look."

Cut into the wall where Roger was standing there was another arched doorway. This one had not been blocked up. But Roger was not pointing at the doorway or the passageway beyond it, where a few steps were visible before the staircase faded upward into darkness.

Water had dripped from cracks in the rock face, trickling down the wall to collect in a pool at the doorway's threshold. Beneath the clear water, a symbol glimmered, silvery metal inlaid in stone.

Mella looked at it blankly.

"Doesn't it look like anything to you?" Roger asked.

"Two triangles and a wavy line?"

"Well, yes. Yes. But . . ."

Mella looked at the pool again. The symbol wavered slightly as the water rippled.

"It's what the dragon told us to watch for," she said.

"It's what?"

"The triangles. Like mountain peaks," she explained, sketching two sharp points in the air with her hand. "And the wavy line, that could be a river. Or a waterfall."

"It could." Roger peered at the symbol, fascinated. "I didn't think of that."

"Then what did you mean?"

"They're signs. Old ones, older than written language. The Defenders have some very old books and scrolls, so I learned the signs to be able to read them. That triangle on the left is fire. The one with the line through it is air. Sometimes it means flight."

"And the wavy line?"

"Well . . . it could be water. Like you said. But with the fork at the end—it means serpent. Snake."

Serpent. Flight. Fire.

"They were breeding something here," Roger said slowly. "But not farm dragons. And that . . ."

He pointed to the wall above the doorway. Mella could just make something out, a worn carving in the stone. A crown with three diamonds above it.

"I've seen that before," she said, puzzled.

"Of course you have." Roger dug a hand in the purse at his belt and pulled something out, a silver coin. "Look here."

On one side, a profile of King Astor. Mella had seen him only once, when his older brother died in battle, leaving him the crown. He'd gone on a progress through his new kingdom, and Mella's father had held her up as the royal procession passed, so that she could see her king.

Roger turned the coin over in his fingers. On

the other side, worn smooth with age and handling, was the crown and three diamonds. The royal family's coat of arms. Each king from Coel on downward had claimed it for his own.

"Coel's sign," Roger said quietly.

Mella shook her head.

"You said it yourself. Coel made the dragons and set them free."

"No." Mella shook her head again. "It's just a rhyme. A game song. It doesn't mean—"

"Are you sure?"

"It doesn't *matter*." Mella shook her head to put away these thoughts. Signs and symbols and children's songs, old coats of arms and people who, too long ago to count the years, had built a bridge and made a stone staircase and carved a cave out of a mountain only to wall it up again, leaving dragons inside to die. It was all a puzzle and a mystery, and she didn't have time for it. "Let's go. Come on."

"Up *there*?"

"Where else? We need to go up, don't we?"

"Wait. Mella, wait a minute—"

"Wait?" She turned back in frustration. "For what?"

Roger knelt to gather up the branches he'd dropped at his feet and pulled the dried moss out of the pouch at his belt, where he'd put it to keep it dry. "For light," he said simply. "Not much use trying to climb up a mountain in the dark."

Chapter Fifteen

Roger ripped a long strip from the bottom of his shirt, wrapped it around the end of a knobby branch, then struck a spark into his tinder and coaxed the flame onto his makeshift torch. Mella, meanwhile, took her wet cloak from her shoulders and wrapped it around the box with the Egg inside it. She tied the corners together to make a sling and settled it over one shoulder, the knot against her chest and the Egg held securely on her back.

Her hands quivered with impatience while she worked. Roger was taking so *long* to get a light burning. But when he was ready at last, she hesitated on the edge of the pool for a moment with an odd reluctance to put her feet in the water.

The symbol—serpent, fire, flight—glimmered beneath the surface of the shallow water, almost as if it gave off its own light. Mella had an uneasy feeling that the faint glow might soak through her skin and seep into her bones. But when she waded in at last, after Roger, the water felt nothing more than freshly cold, quickly soaking through her wet shoes.

The walls of the passageway were rough, unfinished, natural rock. The ceiling was so low that the smoke from Roger's torch hung just over their heads. Once this had been only a narrow crack in the cave wall, nothing more than a tunnel. But someone had carved steps into the floor, and though the tunnel twisted and wound and curved through the rock of the mountain, it continued to go steadily upward.

Soon Mella's calves and knees began to ache. And she was hungry. They hadn't eaten since the few bites they'd shared with Gwyn. Warm oatcakes, Mella thought longingly. Fresh, soft white cheese. Better yet, thick toasted bread with tangy jam, and crisp, salty bacon, and dragon's eggs, light and fluffy and so hot they steamed on your plate. . . .

But they had no food. What they'd had, and it hadn't been much, had been in their packs, which were somewhere back at Gwyn's village. At least she was not cold anymore. Laying a hand against the wall, she found to her surprise that it was warm to the touch. Her hair and clothes dried as they made their way upward.

Gray walls, gray floor, gray ceiling overhead. Mella found herself thinking almost as hungrily about color as about food. Sunlight on a field of yellow and white daisies. The green ribbons in Lilla's hair. Time itself seemed to have gone blank and gray. How long had they been climbing? Without the sun overhead, it was hard to be sure. Their first torch burned down, and Roger lit the second. Then, ahead of Mella, he stopped and bent down. When he turned, he had something in his hand. Silently he held it out to her. It was a lantern, its metal frame eaten into lace by rust. Someone must have tossed it aside when its candle burned down.

Roger suggested a rest and jammed the torch into a crack between stairs. They sat with their backs to a pleasantly warm stone wall. Mella began to wonder if it had been a good idea to sit down. Her legs felt rubbery, her head heavy. Getting up again seemed impossible.

Roger pushed something into her hand. She blinked at it in surprise. It was a chunk of white cheese.

"I put some in my purse," he explained, keeping his voice low. The silence of miles and miles of rock pressed in on them, and it seemed best to be quiet. "Back at the village. Some bread, too." The cheese was coated with lint and dust from the inside of Roger's purse, and the oatcake had crumbled to bits, but Mella's mouth watered eagerly.

"Maybe we should save some," she whispered. "For later. We don't know how long this tunnel is."

Roger shrugged and bit into his own piece of

cheese. "If we're too weak from hunger, we'll never find out. You'd better eat it."

He was probably right. Mella felt her head clear the moment she swallowed. And she remembered that Roger still owed her an explanation.

"What about Alain?" she demanded. "You said you'd tell me."

"Oh." Roger swallowed. "I did tell you. I hit him."

"With a rock." Roger nodded. "That's not telling!" In her impatience, Mella forgot about staying quiet. Her voice bounced back oddly from the rock all around. "What *happened*? Honestly, Roger."

Roger seemed reluctant to talk about it, but under Mella's prodding the story came out. He'd run back through the woods only to find Gwyn, his staff broken at his feet, Alain's sword at his throat. From behind, a well-aimed rock had hit Alain on the back of the skull—and that had been the end of it.

"Really?" Mella beamed. "Good for you."

Roger gave her an astonished look. "Attacking from behind? With a rock? It wasn't exactly . . ." His voice trailed away. "I mean, a knight isn't . . . And if I'd been quicker, Gwyn wouldn't have . . . He was hurt, you know. A bad cut through his shoulder. That's why he dropped the staff, I suppose. He was bleeding."

"And you don't like blood." Mella remembered him saying so. In the smoky orange light from the torch, Roger's face looked thin and pale.

"I bandaged it up. I used pieces from his cloak. I think I stopped the bleeding. But he passed out, all that blood, and then I saw . . ."

"What?" Why did Mella have to drag this story out of Roger one word at a time?

"You saw them too. I didn't stay to chat. I thought I'd better find you. They were close by. They would have found Alain and Gwyn. And Gwyn can explain, when he wakes up. It would have been . . . complicated. If I had stayed."

Just a bit complicated, Mella thought, trying to imagine Roger explaining why he was alone on a mountain slope with two men, both unconscious, one bleeding.

"So I ran. Like a—" Roger's mouth shaped the word *coward*.

Mella stared at him. "You're an idiot," she declared.

Roger's head jerked a little, as if she had slapped him. He looked almost indignant.

"What do you know about it? You're a—you don't know. About knights. About the rules. About everything."

Perhaps it wasn't impossible to pick a fight with Roger after all.

"I know Gwyn would have been dead if you hadn't gone back," Mella pointed out tartly. "I know there's no point attacking a man with a sword from the front if you don't have one yourself. And Alain, of all people . . . Honestly, Roger. If you're worrying about being nice to *him* . . ."

"It's not about being nice," Roger answered hotly. "It's about being, well . . ."

"Noble?" Mella finished for him.

His jaw took on a stubborn set. "Yes."

"Well, then. Isn't it noble to save a life? Isn't it noble not to desert a companion? You had to help Gwyn. The rest is just . . ." Mella waved an impatient hand. "It doesn't matter *how*. It's nice to have a sword and armor and a banner, I suppose, and to do it all prettily, but don't you think Gwyn is glad you went back, no matter what?"

"You don't understand." Roger was shaking his head, but he didn't sound angry anymore. A smile was even tugging at one corner of his mouth.

"I do understand," Mella said with dignity. "I just think you're being stupid."

Roger actually laughed and, swallowing the last mouthful of dry oatcake, he got to his feet. "Come on," he said, reaching down to pull her up as well.

They kept climbing, the tunnel growing narrower and the stairs steeper as they went. Once Mella's foot came down on a slab of rock that crumbled as she touched it, and she slid down several feet before she could catch herself. More than once, piles of rocks, fallen from the ceiling, blocked their way. And once, as Roger climbed over such an obstacle, a light dusting of sand drifted down on his head, and then a few pebbles dropped down around him. He and Mella both froze, holding their breath. But the ceiling held firm.

The second branch Roger had brought burned down. The third. The fourth.

Mella took the fifth torch from Roger's hand and pushed ahead. She didn't want to acknowledge what they both knew—that this was the last one.

She wanted to run, but her legs ached and dragged. The stairs were steeper now, and she had to use her free hand to help herself up.

Mella thought that, if she ever got down to level ground again, she'd never leave it. She'd sleep on the first floor of the Inn. In the kitchen, on the hearth. She'd watch the fire all night, she'd bank it and tend it and clean out the ashes, if only she never had to walk up one more stair.

"Mella. Stop."

She didn't.

"Mella. The torch is burning down."

It wasn't.

"Mella. Look. Your hand."

Her hand had been uncomfortably warm for a while now. She had been ignoring it. But the sharp bite of the fire was suddenly too fierce, and without meaning to she let the torch drop.

The burning brand broke into pieces as it hit the floor. The red coals glowed in the dark and slowly died. Blackness folded in around them. Mella could almost feel it, soft and clinging as cobwebs, brushing against her face. She'd thought the darkness outside, on a moonless night, had been thick. But it had been nothing compared to this.

Roger stumbled against her, grasped her arm.

"Mella? We have to go back."

Roger was right, of course. How could they grope their way forward in pitch blackness? Ahead of them, the stairs might be broken entirely. Fallen rock might block the passageway. Chasms might have opened up in the floor. They couldn't go on, unable to see where they were putting their feet.

But Mella didn't turn around despite the tugging of Roger's persistent hand. She felt like a fish on a hook, being pulled upstream. If she turned back now, the hook would be torn out of her, and she might die from the wound.

But how could she tell that to Roger? She'd sound mad.

"Mella. Come on."

"Look." Mella whispered it.

She might not have seen it if the torch had not gone out: a patch of light, dim with distance, far ahead. It seemed to dance and swim in front of her eyes. She blinked hard. It was still there.

The two of them groped their way toward the light that became steadily brighter and stronger. Soon the stairs flattened out into a gently sloping tunnel, and they ran. When they tumbled out at last into a wide, stony valley, they had to cover their eyes with their hands, shielding their sight from the brilliance of raw sunlight.

At last Mella, blinking away tears, could look up. The valley was no more colorful than the tunnel, a tumbled wasteland of gray rock. But the blue sky, streaked with creamy white clouds, arched high overhead, and Mella sighed with satisfaction to look at it.

The valley was almost perfectly circular, as if they stood inside an enormous bowl, with a dark lake at its center. The gigantic rock formations scattered around were shaped and sculpted by wind. There was nothing jagged about them, everything rounded and smooth.

"A volcano," Roger said, gazing raptly around. "An ancient volcano, it must be. Did you feel how warm the rock was when we were coming up?" He laid his hand against the curve of a gray rock that rose above his head. "Here, too. Volcanic . . . Mella, what is it?"

Mella was looking up, past the walls of the valley. On either side, a pair of matching mountains stood sentinel. Their steep slopes rose to peaks splashed with white.

"The Fangs," she said shakily. "Roger, look where we are. Between the Fangs."

Roger followed her gaze. "*This* is the Hatching Ground?"

Mella spun slowly around to take in the whole of the valley. "It must be. Look—"

She had turned back to face the way they had come, and suddenly her words stuck in her throat.

Where was the entrance to the tunnel? They couldn't be more than a few yards away, yet Mella couldn't see it. They were surrounded on all sides by the smooth, round boulders.

"Roger—" Mella's voice came out faintly. She felt a powerful urge to throw herself into a hole and hide. But where? And from what?

She blinked.

That smell—it had been days now since she'd smelled the familiar whiff of sulfur and ashes. And the rock just in front of her was changing color.

A wash of warm, light brown spread across the dull gray stone. But it didn't stay brown. It brightened every moment until it was the bronze of late sunlight, then the yellow of buttercups, then the brilliant gold of newly minted coins.

At the same time, it moved. A wave of rock shifted and stretched, becoming a shoulder. Another rounded like a back haunch. A long, thin, snakelike neck unwound itself, and a crack in the rock opened and widened until Mella was looking into a deep black eye larger than her head.

All around them, the same thing was happening. Rocks that were not rocks, rocks that were hidden dragons, sat up, their wings stretching to the sky, their unfriendly eyes on Mella and Roger.

"Um, Mella," Roger muttered. "Do you think they—they know? Why we're here?"

The great golden dragon opened her mouth. Her words came out among wisps and curls of steam.

"Trespassers. Humans. This place is forbidden to you."

Mella's tongue was stuck, her jaw stiff. She'd forgotten—how could she forget?—how *big* the true dragons were. And this one was twice the size of the one she had encountered near the Inn. She shrank back a step, until a puff of steam, hot and damp on the back of her neck, made her jump forward again.

"They don't *know*," Roger hissed in her ear.

Well, you tell them! Mella wanted to snap. But she didn't. It was her place. She was the keeper.

"We're not—" she croaked. Oh, that was terrible. She tried again. "We came here—"

The golden dragon's head snaked closer to Mella. Her nostrils flared and her black eyes widened.

"The Egg," she growled. Her tail slapped the ground, scattering stones. "I can smell it. What have you—"

"Yes!" Mella burst out. "We brought it, I promised, here, here it is, we . . ." She yanked at the cloak draped over her shoulder. Her fingers, awkward and clumsy, fumbled with the knots. At last she pushed the rough cloth away and held out the metal box to the dragon. "See, here it—"

But the box was hot, hotter than it had ever been. The scalding heat bit deep into Mella's fingers. She would never have dropped it on purpose, but her hands simply wouldn't hold it. She gasped. Roger let out a cry and fell to his knees, trying to catch the box, but he was too late. It hit the stony ground with a sharp crack.

Mella nearly shrieked, but the sound caught in her throat, sharp as ice.

"Oh, no," Roger whispered. "Oh, no, Mella, look . . ."

The lid of the box had sprung open when it hit the ground. Inside, Mella could see the Egg, a network of fine cracks webbed across its surface.

"It's broken. Mella, it's broken."

Mella felt a broad grin spread across her face. She looked up into the dark eyes of the golden dragon.

"No," she said. "It's hatching."

Chapter Sixteen

The next few moments were very confusing.

The golden dragon pounced. Roger flinched, and Mella yelped, but the dragon ignored them, only scooping the Egg up tenderly in her long, curved black claws. As though in a cage, it lay cradled in them, quivering with the energy of the hatchling inside.

The golden wings spread wide, and the sun glowed through them. Then the wings swept down, and the dragon was aloft. Mella and Roger ducked down as she flew over their heads toward the center of the valley. The other dragons followed, their wings stirring up a storm of wind that tugged at Mella's skirts and showered her with dust and grit and tiny pebbles. In seconds the two humans were alone.

The mouth of the tunnel they had come through was visible now, a crack between two slabs of stone.

"Maybe we should . . ." Roger nodded at the black hole in the mountainside.

"But it's *hatching*!" Mella stood up. The valley that had seemed bare and lifeless before was alive with dragons, all flying or leaping over rocks and boulders toward the dark lake in the center. "Don't you want to *see*?"

"Not if I get eaten for it!"

It was very sensible, Mella knew. One dragon in the woods near the Inn had been frightening enough. Here was a whole valley full of them. And they'd already been told that they had no right to be here.

But—the Egg was hatching. *Her* Egg. The Egg she had left her home and herd for. The Egg she'd saved. How could she leave now?

"Pardon me." The low, hissing voice near her

elbow made Mella jump. A dragon sidled around a boulder to peer at them. He had creamy white scales and eyes of a clear, amber brown.

"You are the human children who brought the Egg?"

Mella nodded. This dragon was much smaller than the golden one, smaller even than the gray green dragon near the Inn. But it was still quite big enough to bite off her head, or Roger's, if it chose.

"Well, then." The white dragon's tail beat a quick rhythm in the gravel. "Well, well, well . . ."

It was clearly torn by indecision. Its wings quivered eagerly, and its amber eyes darted from Mella to Roger to the lake at the valley's center, where the golden form of the huge dragon could be seen glowing in the sun.

"Then come," the white dragon said, seeming to make up its mind. "Join me. The Hatching—I cannot wait—but you should witness." He dipped his neck low to the ground and crouched. "I am Alyas. Hurry!"

Mella and Roger shared a glance. There was the safety of the tunnel behind them. But there was Alyas, waiting—and the Egg, hatching.

"Come on," Mella said roughly, as if Roger were delaying them. "He said to hurry!"

She stepped as lightly as she could on Alyas's bent knee and threw one leg across his shoulders, just where the neck joined the body. Roger scrambled up behind her. She felt Alyas's muscles tense as he crouched even lower and jumped into the air. He grunted. His wings beat frantically. He was quite a small dragon, Mella realized. The two of them together made a heavy burden for him.

Then Alyas gained some height, his wing beats steadied, and they were soaring toward the lake.

Dragons were thronging the sky, in all the colors that Mella remembered from her own herd—lichen green, tawny brown, soft gray, glossy black. A few were white like Alyas. Only one, the dragon that had taken the Egg, was golden; none of the others were as big.

Alyas made good use of his small size, darting

between larger dragons. Mella was thrown forward along his neck as he dove toward the ground, and Roger clutched her from behind with a startled "Oof!" With a deft turn, Alyas glided in to claim the last open space in a ring of dragons by the lake shore.

Mella and Roger tumbled off Alyas's back. The golden dragon crouched in the center of the ring, the Egg still clutched in her claws. Carefully, she laid it down in the center of a circle of smooth black rock. As the dragon backed away, Mella saw, inlaid in the rock, the same symbol she had seen below, the two triangles with the wavy line beneath them. Flight, fire, serpent. Dragon.

The Egg rocked. Mella's breath got stuck somewhere behind her breastbone. She found she was holding Roger's hand, squeezing tightly enough to hurt.

The strange symbol, made of a dull silvery metal laid into grooves in the rock, began to brighten. At first Mella thought it was a trick of her eye or a stray beam of sunlight. She blinked.

But the symbol glowed steadily brighter and brighter, its shine rippling across the glossy scales of the dragons and sparkling in their eyes. Mella glanced aside at Roger's face and saw it washed in pearly light.

Then the symbol flashed, for an instant seeming brighter than the sun. Mella had to close her eyes. When she opened them again, blinking away tears, the Egg had fallen open. A tiny golden dragon tumbled and rolled among the glistening black eggshells, a snarl of legs and wings and neck and tail.

Mella's hands ached to hold her, to steady her and help her stand, to carefully stretch the damp wings to the sunlight, as she would have done with a chick from her own herd. Beside her she heard Roger let out his breath slowly in a long "ah."

"A queen," Alyas breathed. "A queen!"

All over the valley the dragons roared, sitting back on their hind legs, lashing their tails. Some leaped to the skies to soar in great loops, their wings casting shadows that flickered over Roger and Mella and the dragons still on the ground. Even the chick joined in, stretching her neck out and roaring as well. It sounded like an avalanche and a thunderstorm together, and Mella and Roger had to cover their ears, huddling down as the sound crashed and boomed around them.

At last the tumult died away. The newborn dragon, frantic with delight, scampered toward the great golden one. She must be the leader, Mella decided, cautiously uncovering her ears and straightening up. The queen. And this chick would be the next queen. She would grow up to rule.

The queen dragon swooped her head down to touch noses with the chick and then gently scooped her up under one wing. Mella felt an ache swell up inside her like a bitter, salty wave. She should have been happy. She'd done what she'd promised. She'd brought the Egg safely to the Hatching Ground. She'd done a keeper's job.

But now that job was over. Now she was just a keeper far from her own herd, with nothing to watch over.

"Alyas." The voice rumbled, deep and threatening, across the Hatching Ground. "What are you doing with those *humans*? What business have humans here?"

The speaker was a large dragon, his scales the russet brown of oak leaves in the winter. His neck arched now so that the crest along it stood up threateningly. He was at least twice Alyas's size.

"Ah." Alyas blinked nervously. "I thought . . . that is, considering . . . it seemed to me . . ."

"To *you*!" The brown dragon's voice rose scornfully. "It seemed good to *you* that these should witness a Hatching?"

"Peace, Chiath." The golden dragon turned an eye sternly on the brown one. "We will not mar the Hatching with a quarrel." Mella let out a shaky breath, relieved. But then the queen swiveled her head to transfer her glare to the small white dragon. "Alyas. You take much upon yourself."

"Pardon, my queen." Alyas dipped his head in a quick, obsequious gesture. His crest lay flat along his neck, and he seemed to be trying to look as harmless as possible. "I thought . . ."

"You thought to bring humans here," Chiath hissed. "When none have set foot on the Hatching Ground since the days of Coel the Traitor. Outsiders. Trespassers!"

"We are not!" Dragon or not, Mella decided, she didn't like Chiath. He was just like Blackie in her own herd, bullying the smaller dragons. "We were *asked* to come here," she continued angrily, chin up, fist clenched at her sides. "We were *asked* to bring the Egg."

"Mella!" Roger breathed urgently in her ear.

"Asked?" The queen tipped her head slightly to take in both Roger and Mella with one dark eye. "And who asked you to do so? It was Kieron who was sent to bring the Egg here. We have waited two days, but he did not arrive."

Too late, Mella understood Roger's warning. Should she tell this circle of dragons, some looking easily as hostile as Chiath, that they had been asked to deliver the Egg by a dying dragon, killed by a dragon-slayer?

The dragons waited, their eyes on Mella and Roger. The long claws on Alyas's front feet scratched anxiously at the gravel on the ground. They all had claws like that, Mella thought. Maybe she and Roger should have bolted for the safety of the tunnel when they'd had the chance. Claws and teeth and breath of fire . . .

"My sorrow, but Kieron will not return," Roger said clearly, stepping forward. "He was slain."

Mella glanced at him in alarm. Surely he would not confess to being a Defender's squire? She broke in quickly before Roger could be overcome by an attack of honesty. For all she knew, it might be something to do with those rules of honor he was overly concerned with obeying. "But before he died, he told us where to come," she said. "He gave the Egg to us."

No one spoke. Mella did not know how long the silence lasted. She was watching the queen dragon, and she felt as if those black eyes were pools deeper than the earth's core. Dizzy, she seemed to be standing on the very edge.

"For long now, humans have been our enemies," the queen said at last. Chiath hissed in agreement, and she cast him a quelling glance. "But it was not always so. Once every hundred years an Egg is laid, and it can only hatch here, where the first of our kind broke free of their shells. If this one had been lost, great would have been our sorrow. We are in your debt."

Alyas let out a long sigh, hissing through his nostrils in relief. To Mella's surprise, Roger made the dragon queen a formal and elegant bow. She followed his lead and bobbed a curtsy.

"I am Roger Astorson and this is Mella Evasdaughter," Roger said. He sounded quite dignified. "We are glad to have been of service."

The queen looked as if she might have said more, but a harsh-edged roar from far above made everyone look up. It came from one of the dragons that had taken to the sky earlier, and the alarm in his voice was clear to Mella—her herd would roar so, in challenge and warning, when they heard a hunting cat howl from the woods.

Now the beast plunged out of the sky, its wings close to its body. Mella thought it had been hurt somehow and expected another to leap to its aid, but the dragon's wings snapped out when it was not far above their heads, and he landed deftly in the center of the circle, next to the silver symbol in the rock and the shards of eggshell. His scales were glossy black, his wings smoky gray, and his crest rippling up and down in agitation.

"Humans! Humans marching! They've come *here*! A human army on the plain below us!"

"I knew it!" Chiath bellowed, swinging his head toward Roger and Mella. "They have led an army here!"

The air around Mella seethed with growls and hisses and roars and angry words. Chiath's neck arched, his crest bristling, and his mouth opened. Roger grabbed Mella's arm. But there was nothing he could do, nowhere to run, no words they could speak that would be heard above the clamor. She looked around wildly and saw that Alyas had retreated several paces and was trying to look as if the two human children had nothing to do with him.

In a moment they would be dead, Mella thought, burned to ash, and all because of an army they knew nothing about. And what was an army doing here, of all places? Then a quick flash of memory came to her, of sunlight on polished metal, something red and yellow shaken like a curtain in the wind—a banner? But it made no sense, no sense at all, and now she was going to die for it. And Roger too. Poor Roger. She was sorry she'd dragged him to see the Hatching, sorry she'd brought him on this quest at all, sorry she'd made him fetch the Egg from under her bed so long ago.

Chiath's mouth opened wider, the dark tongue flexing, the long fangs bright white in the sun.

And then a streak of gold dashed across the dark sand of the Hatching Ground. The little dragon chick had wriggled her head out from under the queen's wing and squirmed loose to run to her human keeper. Mella knelt and held out her arms, and the chick leapt onto her lap. Turning to face the other dragons, the chick braced her front claws on Mella's knees and chattered high-pitched defiance at her kin.

Chiath's mouth snapped shut.

"Peace!" the queen roared, her voice rising above the rest. Her lashing tail smacked into a boulder and cracked it in two. No dragon made a sound except the chick. Tiny crest up, tail thumping against Mella's ribs, she hissed and even puffed out a tiny cloud of steam.

"Shhh," Mella whispered, lifting a hand that trembled slightly to stroke the dragon's neck and scratch behind her ears. Shakily she got to her feet, hugging the chick to her. The little animal felt as warm and light as a loaf of bread fresh from the oven. Mella hoped Roger would have the sense to stay close to the two of them.

"We didn't bring anyone here," Mella said, trying to keep her voice steady. "If there's really an army down there, it's got nothing to do with us."

Beside her, Roger cleared his throat. "Actually," he said hoarsely.

Every pair of eyes, dragon and human, turned to him.

"I think," he said, and paused. "I think they're probably looking for me."

Chapter Seventeen

"An army?" Mella demanded. "Looking for *you*?"

They were by themselves in front of the queen, beside the great dark lake. "I would speak to these humans alone," the huge dragon had said, and the others had promptly and obediently moved away, Chiath with an angry snarl and Alyas with several backward glances.

"It's not really an army," Roger said awkwardly. "I mean, it can't be. There wouldn't have been time to muster the whole army. One company at most. I supposed they followed us. Damien must have sent a message to my . . ." To Mella's astonishment, Roger turned bright red. He finished his sentence with a mumbled word too low for her to hear.

Dragons, however, had very keen ears. "Your *father*?" the queen growled.

"Your—" Mella had to try twice to get the word out. "Your father? Has an *army*?"

But of course he did. Roger had told her so himself not three minutes ago. "Roger Astorson," he'd said. The youngest son of King Astor.

Mella was outraged. "You never *said*!"

Roger looked ready to melt with embarrassment. "I didn't think he'd *come*," he mumbled. "He's busy. There's so much to do."

"You didn't think he'd come when his *son* disappeared?"

Roger shrugged miserably. Mella shook her head. "So that's why Alain . . ."

"He must have spent some time in the capital," Roger said glumly. "He probably saw me there."

"You could have said!"

"I didn't want . . ."

"And what's he *doing*?"

The queen had been listening attentively. But now she spoke, and her crest bristled ominously. "What he is doing," she said, low and fierce, "is fairly obvious. He is going to war."

"Against the dragons," Mella said, understanding at last. "Because he thinks they . . . took his son? The prince," Mella added pointedly. "You."

The queen and Roger both nodded. They had grasped what was happening, Mella realized, much more quickly than she had.

Roger lifted his head to look the dragon queen in the eye. "You must let us go down," he said quickly. "It's the only thing to do."

"Must I?" The deep black eye of the dragon opened a little wider, and her voice was soft. Mella nearly shivered, and without meaning to she clutched the dragon chick a little closer. That soft voice and that thoughtful eye were much more frightening than Chiath's roar.

"You are no prince here," the queen said quietly to Roger. "Do not presume."

"I do not."

This was Roger? Mella blinked in surprise at his sharp tone. She'd heard him sound like this only once before, when he'd confronted Alain. When had he learned to sound this sure of himself?

"I do not presume," Roger said, more softly this time. "They are looking for me. If they see I'm safe, they won't attack. It's best for all of us if we both go down."

The queen closed her eyes briefly and then opened them again. Slowly she shook her great golden head from side to side. "You know the way to the Hatching Ground," she said, her deep voice rumbling in Mella's bones. "That is something the human army must not know."

"We wouldn't *tell*!" Mella said indignantly.

"We cannot take that risk," answered the queen. "We will not harm you. But we cannot let you leave."

"We—we saved the Egg for you!" Mella felt as if her anger were fizzing and spurting inside of her. "We brought it all the way here, and—" *And it wasn't easy!* she wanted to shout. There'd been

miles of walking, a river, a kidnapper, the darkness inside a mountain. But they'd done it. They'd
made it. And this was the gratitude they got?
"You said you were in our debt!" Mella shouted in
outrage, and the dragon chick chattered like a
frightened squirrel and fanned her delicate golden
wings.

"Mella!" Roger snapped, and Mella realized
belatedly that yelling at a queen might not be the
wisest course when they stood in a valley surrounded by dragons. But the queen did not seem
angry.

"And so we are," she said, and dipped her head
to Mella. "In debt to both of you. And if it were my
danger and my choice only, I would carry you
down myself. You have earned as much. But a
queen has more to think of than her honor. I
cannot risk the safety of us all."

"But sending us down will only serve the safety
of your people—dragons—subjects," Roger argued,
much more politely than Mella. "The army will
have scouts in the forest. They might find the way

up at any moment, and even if they don't—" He swept a hand at the stony valley. "You cannot stay here forever. If you manage to fly off under cover of night, they'll follow you. Now that they know you exist, they'll hunt you. You won't be able to hide anymore."

"We do not *hide* from humans," the queen growled.

"Forgive me for the word, then. But my father's army will find you."

"And if they do, do you think we cannot fight them?"

"Of course you can," Roger agreed readily. "But he can afford to lose much more than you can. The wolf is stronger, but the dogs still bring it down. You don't need a war. You need a treaty. And we can make one for you."

The dragon chick squirmed in Mella's arms, and she let the little creature down gently to the pebbly ground. The queen and Roger—the queen and the prince—seemed to have forgotten she was there.

"I will not say to you that humans have no honor,"

the queen said, giving Roger a long, steady glance. "But we have been betrayed in the past. And your blood is—"

"Is *what*?"

"It is not easy for any dragon to trust one of Coel's house. You came up by the old passageway. Did what you saw there tell you no tales?"

"What we saw there?" Roger's brow furrowed. "We saw—we didn't understand what we saw. Dragons and . . . bones . . . we don't know . . ."

"Humans have short lives and short memories. You do not know what you ask, when you ask me for my trust."

"Then keep me."

Mella was surprised to hear the words coming out of her own mouth.

"What?" Roger stared at her. The queen did as well.

Mella cleared her throat. "You can keep me. As a hostage. If Roger—if the army doesn't leave—then you can . . ." Maybe it would be best, she thought, not to finish that sentence.

Roger looked alarmed. "That's—Mella, I don't think that's—"

The queen laughed. The ground trembled under Mella's feet.

"Now we must both trust. Is that it? No one told me humans were such clever bargainers. Well done. One may stay and one may go. And you, prince, have told us time is short. You will go now."

It would take too long, the queen had said, for Roger to return by the staircase, and she chose a young dragon with bronze-colored scales to carry him down instead.

"And Lynet will take you," the queen had told Mella.

Take her? Mella had thought she was staying. She'd thought that was the whole point. "Take me where?"

"Somewhere safe," was all the queen had answered.

Lynet turned out to be a gray dragon with the small crest of a female. With Mella on her back and Roger on the bronze, they stood at the very edge of the valley. Mella, peering down, saw a sheer wall plummeting to a valley hundreds of feet below, where a frothy white river churned and leaped through its bed. She turned her head to look at Roger. There had hardly been time to speak before the queen had ordered them on dragonback. She should have said good-bye, or good luck, or something. Roger's mouth was moving, but the wind whipping past her ears snatched the sound away.

Then Lynet fell forward.

She did not leap, she simply toppled like a stone. It happened so quickly that Mella felt her body rise off the dragon's back, and she threw herself forward to clamp both arms around the smooth gray neck. She thought she might have screamed, but they were falling too swiftly for her own voice to reach her ears.

Lynet did not even flap her wings. She simply held them out to each side, fully extended, as they fell.

And then they hit the updraft the dragon had been expecting. Mella was crushed down by the pressure as they suddenly soared upward.

The bronze dragon swooped down, hidden from the sight of the army by a long outcropping of stone. But Lynet didn't follow. She swerved to the left and landed deftly on a wide stony ledge that jutted out from the mountain, beating her wings for balance and scattering pebbles widely.

The dragon twisted her head on her long, flexible neck so that she could look coldly at Mella, still seated on her back. "The queen has said you are to wait here," she said shortly.

Here? This was somewhere safe? Mella climbed down very carefully, keeping the dragon's body between herself and the sheer drop. The ledge was wide enough that there was no real danger of falling as long as she watched where she put her feet. All the same, she felt better after she'd sat down with her back firmly against the mountainside.

"How long?" she asked.

But Lynet didn't seem inclined to waste words on her human passenger. She spread her wings and leaped off the ledge—Mella pressed herself harder against the rocky wall behind her and covered her face with her hands as the dragon's wing beats stirred up a small whirlwind—and then swooped back up to the valley, leaving Mella alone.

From the ledge, Mella could see the river they had toiled up so painfully, a silver chain curling across the gray and green land. She could even see the waterfall that had marked the entrance to the mysterious room and the stairway up the mountain. On the plain beside the pool where she had fallen in, she could see something else—rows and rows of dull white squares stretched across the grass. Tents, Mella realized. Bright streamers snapped in the wind. The largest tent, in the middle, was not white, but striped red and yellow.

So that was what an army looked like.

Mella watched tiny scurrying shapes, small and urgent as ants, hurrying among the patches of white. She watched clouds scroll and drift across the bright blue sky. An eagle flew past, so far below that she could look down on its strong brown wings. She supposed that never before had a prisoner had such a breathtaking view.

But the ledge was still a prison. No way up or down, nothing she dared to climb, nothing to do but wait.

Chapter Eighteen

Sitting on her ledge, Mella counted two more eagles and four hawks before something bigger than either came flying toward her, wings glimmering white in the sunlight. Alyas landed awkwardly on the ledge, scattering pebbles, flapping his wings wildly for balance. He was having trouble, Mella realized, because he was holding something in one clawed forefoot, something heavy and limp that dripped red onto the ground.

Mella stifled the screech that rose up in her throat. Whatever he was holding was definitely . . . dead.

"Venison. I thought you must be hungry," Alyas explained politely, holding the haunch of meat out to her. "Some of us had been hunting before you arrived. I like cooked meat, myself. But do you prefer it raw?"

"Cooked is fine, thank you," Mella said, her voice just the slightest bit quivery and wavering with relief.

Alyas turned his head aside, cleared his throat—a rumbling sound that started deep in his chest and traveled slowly up his long neck—opened his mouth, and directed a stream of flame at the raw meat, turning it carefully on one claw as it roasted. The rich smell made Mella's stomach growl and for a moment it took her back to the Inn, with meat turning on the spit before the fire, ready to feed the hungry guests who would be arriving soon. She had to blink hard to keep from crying. How had she gotten from her home to this windswept ledge on a mountainside, sharing a meal with a dragon? And would she ever get back?

Since Mella had no knife—it had been taken from her at Gwyn's village—Alyas used his claws to cut slices of the meat for her. It was roasted to a turn—crisp on the outside, pink inside, and dripping juices over Mella's burnt fingers. Hunger won out over homesickness and worry, and Mella ate with single-minded devotion until her stomach was satisfied at last. She sighed and wiped her mouth on her sleeve.

Alyas had settled down on his haunches and tucked his tail around himself, neat as a cat. He offered Mella something else, something she had not noticed before—a small skin of fresh water. "The queen has said you must be cared for," he remarked as she drank thirstily. "She said that we must treat you as a friend until the worst is proved."

Mella lowered the water skin. "Nothing's going to be proved," she said angrily. "Roger *said*."

Roger had, after all, defeated Alain. He'd rescued the Egg when she'd dropped it. If he said he could turn an army around, she would believe him.

Alyas's crest rippled up and down nervously.

"I hope so. For both our sakes. No one will let me forget that I befriended humans."

Mella frowned. "Well, the people I know are not likely to be very happy that I saved a dragon's egg," she pointed out. *But I'm not keeping you trapped on a ledge because of it*, she didn't add. She felt that her pointed silence was eloquent enough.

Alyas sighed. The wind of it blew Mella's hair into her eyes. She felt her face settling down into a sulky expression.

Far below, another eagle screamed. The sound died away.

Mella brushed a flat stretch of the ledge clean of pebbles and dirt and then selected ten small stones, five dark, five light. With a sharp-edged rock she scratched a grid on the rock with two lines one way, two the other.

"Here," she said, pushing the dark pebbles over toward Alyas. "You try to get three in a row. I'll go first."

Mella won the first two games, Alyas the third. After that it became too easy. Mella made the grid wider, and they played at four in a row, then five. Alyas bent close over the game board. He tended to puff small clouds of steam from his nostrils when he was thinking.

Mella leaned over to place her third stone. "Why did you, then?" she asked.

"I beg your pardon? Why did I . . . ?"

"Befriend humans." There must have been some reason, after all, why Alyas had approached them, why he'd taken them to see the Hatching, why he alone of all the dragons seemed willing to talk to them.

The tip of Alyas's tail twitched, brushing a few pebbles off the ledge. "Well, I . . . that is . . ." He picked up a pebble between two claws and put it neatly in place. "Perhaps you would not mind . . ."

"Mind what?" She'd win, Mella thought, if he left that there. He wasn't paying attention to the game.

"Would you care to . . . to tell me . . ."

"Tell you *what*?"

"Your story!" Alyas exclaimed, as if it should

have been obvious. "The rescue of the Egg! I am, you see, a song-maker." His wings lifted off his back and flapped slightly, stirring a breeze that blew dust and grit into Mella's face. "If it is true . . . I mean, well." His crest drooped, and he looked a bit ashamed of himself. "If the other, the boy, does as he promised, if you are truly not spies—"

"You think we're *spies*?" Mella demanded.

Alyas's sigh tumbled the pebbles from their places on the grid. "I do not *think* so. You are only children, after all. And what army would send children as spies? But humans . . . I've always been told how easily humans lie. Still, if you are what you say, if you have saved the Egg through hardship and danger—what a song that would make! Will you tell me?"

"Why should I?" Mella snapped. "Why do you want to hear it? If humans are liars." She didn't have to talk to him just to be insulted, she thought, and sat back against the rock wall, her arms folded.

Alyas looked at her humbly with his brown gold

eyes. "Pardon for offending you. I spoke carelessly. But . . ." His voice took on a coaxing tone. "Do you not wish it known, the truth of how you brought the Egg to us? You and the boy. Coel's son." Coel's great-great-great-great grandson, more like, Mella thought, but didn't bother correcting him. "If Coel's house helped to save an Egg, that would do much to balance the debt between your kind and ours. His name and yours will be remembered by dragons for all time! And of course . . ." He tried to look modest and failed utterly. "Mine as well. As the bard who made the song."

Just to be contrary, Mella made him wheedle a little more. But at length she told him the story. The Egg in the fire and her promise to Kieron. (She admitted that Kieron had been killed by a Defender but neglected to add that the Defender had been Roger's master; no need to give *every* detail.) Alyas growled in appreciation as he heard how the little wild dragons had rescued them from Alain. Gwyn's village and Alain again, the waterfall and the pool and the passageway up through miles of rock. Alyas listened attentively and asked eager questions as the sun slid past its highest point and began the long slide down the other side of the sky.

When she had finished, Alyas made a rumbling sound of appreciation. He seemed to be thinking deeply.

His turn to tell a story now, Mella decided. Why were the dragons so angry at humans? Why did they call Coel a traitor? Gwyn had said something about that as well, about a great betrayal. And did their reason have anything to do with the diamonds of Coel's house carved in the stone before the staircase that led to the Hatching Ground?

But as she drew in a breath to ask the question, a sound interrupted her. It came from high over-head, drifting over the edge of the valley and down to the ledge where she and Alyas sat together.

It was not a roar, or a growl, or a hiss, or any of the sounds Mella was used to from dragons. It was music. If there were words in it, she could not understand them. But the sound was sad and sweet and fierce all at once, and it made her think of the wind before a wild storm and the cold depths of the sky on a winter's night.

"What is it?" she whispered to Alyas.

"It is a lament," the white dragon said softly, blinking his amber eyes. "For Kieron."

Mella could not ask questions then, could not stir, could do nothing but listen, her mind drifting on a river of sound. The song went on and on. It contained, Alyas whispered, all the names of Kieron's ancestors since the first true dragons had hatched.

At last the sound lulled Mella into a sleepy trance. She hadn't slept much the night before, between worrying over the Egg and escaping from Gwyn's village and fleeing from Alain. Not to mention walking up a mountain. She curled up on the ground and her cheek came to rest on something scaly and soft and warm. Alyas tucked a wing snugly over her. She heard a deep rumbling and felt it through her skin as he hummed quietly to himself, working on his song.

Something jerked Mella awake, a long, clear note that might have come from the mouth of a trumpet or the throat of a dragon. She sat up quickly, her head still muzzy with sleep.

"What?" she asked groggily. "What's happening?"

"Amazing," Alyas breathed. He was stretching his long neck out into thin air, peering down at the foot of the mountain.

"*What's* amazing?" Mella, on her hands and knees, crawled out to look over the edge too.

"He has done it. The army is retreating."

And indeed, Mella, squinting in the rising wind, could see that some of the white squares were disappearing even as she watched, being taken down, rolled up, and packed away into parcels too small to be seen from so far above. A line of horses and carts was forming, heading away from the waterfall and the pool.

The anxiety that Mella had been refusing to let herself feel melted away. "I *told* you," she said, feeling a smile stretch wide across her face. "Now you can take me down."

Alyas shook his head. "Now I must take you to the queen. She has said so, indeed." He crouched down so she could climb on his back. "Hold tight."

This time Mella was prepared for a plunge off the ledge, and hugged his neck tightly until his wings caught an updraft to send them soaring back up toward the Hatching Ground.

The queen was waiting for them once more by the lake. And around her, in a circle a respectful distance away, were rows and rows of dragons. Their wings overlapped, and their long necks stretched and strained as they peered overhead to catch a glimpse of Alyas, spiraling down with Mella on his back. She suspected him of adding some graceful turns and flourishes to his descent, purely for drama.

The white dragon landed neatly in front of the queen and dipped his neck in an elegant movement that Mella decided must be the dragon equivalent of a bow. She slipped off his back. One of her feet hit the ground first and the second followed a few moments later, so she had to hop awkwardly to keep her balance. It was the very opposite of graceful, and Mella felt her face blush hot. What was she doing here, alone before a dragon queen? Roger was used to the company of royalty. He would have known what to do or say. Without him, Mella felt grubby and insignificant and extremely small.

However, Roger was *not* there, so she would have to do the best she could without him. Remembering how her friend had bowed, she made the dragon queen a curtsy.

And the queen, with the little dragon chick frisking around her feet, dipped her neck in response.

Had the queen just *bowed* to her, to an innkeeper's daughter? Mella made sure her mouth didn't drop open in astonishment. But she couldn't stop her eyes from widening.

"We are once more in your debt," the dragon queen said.

And all the dragons, even Chiath, gave a muted roar of agreement and approval. They kept the sound low, Mella realized, to spare her ears. But she felt it making the air tremble, vibrating the ground beneath her feet. The breeze of it lifted and stirred her hair.

The queen held her front foot out to Mella. Dangling from a claw were two thin leather thongs. From each swung an ivory white tooth longer than Mella's finger.

"A gift for you and for your companion," the queen said. "These will mark you as dragonfriends. They are yours to wear for life and to pass on to your children."

Every dragon watched as Mella walked across the black sand and reached up to take the two pendants from the queen's claws. She had to blink and squint as the sunlight flashed bright on the queen's golden scales. The dragon towered over her, massive, like a mountain herself—the strong curve of her neck, crowned with her elegant crest, the long slope of her back, the graceful curl of her tail. Mella longed to touch the warmth of those scales, to smooth the crest or rub behind the ears, as she would have done with one of her own herd. But she did not dare. Instead she took the two pendants carefully in her hand, slipping them both over her head for safekeeping.

"Thank you," she said. That was all she could think of. And it seemed to be all that was needed.

The dragon chick had noticed Mella by now, and with chirps of delight pranced over to nibble on the girl's bootlaces and put her small clawed forefeet on Mella's knees. Mella bent down and picked her up, warm in her hands, impossibly light, her scales smooth as water. Fire and air and serpent, Mella thought. Dragon.

The chick nuzzled Mella beneath the chin and hummed with pleasure. Mella didn't want to put her down, even when she squirmed and flapped her wings restlessly. But she did, and the young dragon scampered back toward the queen, who tucked her safely under one wing.

"She is young," the queen said tolerantly. "But

she will come to know how two human children saved her."

Was there something like sympathy in those wide, dark eyes? Could the queen know how Mella felt, how much she missed the weight and the warmth of the Egg in her hands and the knowledge that she was its keeper?

It was hard to tell, looking up at that smooth, scaly face. All the queen said was "Alyas will take you home."

Foolishness, Mella told herself fiercely, blinking hard. She'd brought the Egg here safely. She kept her promise. And now her own herd, as well as her family, were waiting for her back at the Inn. She still had a keeper's job to do, the job Gran had given her.

Gran had known so much, Mella thought. More than Mella would ever learn. But Gran had never known what it was like to talk to a true dragon face-to-face. She'd never flown on dragonback. She'd never heard a dragon sing.

Maybe Mella would never be the keeper Gran

had been. But that did not mean she could not learn to be the keeper she was meant to be herself.

"Not too close to the army," the queen told Alyas. "Keep your distance. And quickly now. We want to show the humans our goodwill."

Chapter Nineteen

On Alyas's back as he perched on the edge of the valley, Mella tucked the two dragontooth pendants carefully inside the neck of her dress. Then she threw herself forward, hugging Alyas's neck as the dragon toppled forward, squeezing her eyes shut so that she didn't have to watch the cliff face hurtling by.

But when their flight steadied, she settled back and sat up once more. She could feel the muscles of the dragon's back working beneath her legs and hands. The rush of cold air stung her eyes, but she kept them open as she leaned over to see the spread of the land below.

There was the army of Roger's father, rows of horses and wagons and columns of marching men, the light catching on their spears and helmets, banners and pennants flashing red and yellow as they marched away from the mountain. Only one tent was left in the grassy plain beside the waterfall—the biggest, with its colorful stripes glowing bright in the sun.

Mella spotted Gwyn's village, the stone crofts and pens blending into the mountainside. She even thought she could glimpse Dragonsford, a dark smudge on the horizon, and a faint gray, wavering line across the distant sky she imagined might be the smoke from the Inn's chimneys.

Then Alyas angled toward a high hill near the plain where the army had camped. It had a bare, rocky outcropping on top where he could land, tucking his wings in neatly to keep from snagging them on the tree branches. Stiff and chilled from the wind, Mella slid awkwardly down.

"I cannot linger," Alyas said, bringing his face close to Mella's. He breathed out a steamy, sulfur-smelling breath and touched Mella's cheek briefly with his hot tongue.

Mella's throat hurt as she put her hands for a

moment to either side of Alyas's face. Her last true dragon. Oh, there was her own herd, waiting at home for her. But for the first time—and she felt a guilty flicker at the disloyal thought—the common farm dragons did not seem quite enough.

"Good-bye," she whispered to Alyas. "I hope your song is famous."

"It should be." Alyas gave a low chuckle that blew Mella's hair back from her face. "With two such heroes, indeed, it should be sung for thousands of years."

Alyas's leap carried him as high as the treetops, and his pale wings beat furiously. Clearly launching from the ground was not as easy as diving from a height. Mella held her breath until the white dragon began to gain altitude. The frantic wing beats slowed to a steady pace, and he swooped up into the sky just as Roger burst through the trees.

"You're all right?" he panted. "I mean, I knew you would be. I saw Alyas flying. I'm sorry it took so long. I had to explain and explain. He couldn't even decide if he was angry—"

A furious bellow came rising up behind him. "My prince!"

Somebody was certainly angry, Mella thought, as a small crowd of people clambered out of the trees and after Roger.

"My prince!" the foremost of these repeated. "You must *not* run ahead like that, and near a *dragon,* of all things! Are you mad?"

"Wiltain," Roger said patiently, "I only wanted to see if Mella was all right. There was no danger."

"There was a *dragon*!" Wiltain wheezed. A portly man, dressed in a long wine-colored velvet coat over his linen shirt, he didn't look as if scrambling through a rocky wood was something he was accustomed to.

There were other people around now, some as finely dressed as Wiltain, others in the plain leather and linen of soldiers, and all of them talking at once.

"My prince, you really must—"

"Impossible to guard you if—"

"Reckless and foolish—"

"They're from my father's court," Roger said in Mella's ear. "Wiltain's the minister of taxation, he really shouldn't have come along on a military campaign at all, but you can't keep him out of anything. That's Owen, he's the captain of my father's guard, and the rest of them, well, they just came along. People do. You *are* all right, aren't you, Mella? I wanted—"

"My prince," the man named Owen interrupted. The soldiers around him, Mella noticed, had bolts readied on their crossbows and were looking nervously at the sky, where Alyas was now a creamy dot against the blue.

"You must not leave your guards," Owen continued reproachfully. "And you must come back with us now. Your father is waiting."

Roger had his chin up and was looking dignified again. "I told you, Owen, there is no danger."

"Nevertheless." Owen stood firm. "You'll return with us now."

The soldiers made a ring around Mella and Roger and Wiltain and the few others whose clothes marked them as nobles, and hurried them back down through the trees and toward the plain. As they climbed over rocks and ducked under branches, Roger kept up a quick stream of commentary, low enough that only Mella could hear.

"He'd arrested Alain *and* Gwyn, can you believe it? Alain because Gwyn said he'd tried to kidnap us, and Gwyn because he wouldn't say where we'd gone, or what he knew, or anything. He's let him go now, of course. I think he might make him a knight. Damien's there too. The healer said he shouldn't ride, but he wouldn't stay behind. I think he's angry, I'm not sure, it's hard to tell sometimes. And now—"

They were at the bottom of the hill, pushing between the last trees and out into the plain beside the waterfall. The flattened grass and trampled mud showed where the army had been. Now there was nothing left of them but what had been dropped or abandoned in the hasty retreat—a tent peg, a scrap of frayed rope, half a loaf of bread ground into the mud, a thrown horseshoe, a stray glove. The soldiers hurried them toward the red and yellow tent, its stripes bright and brave in the sun.

All the other tents Mella had seen from her perch on the mountainside had been plain and white. This one was special. It must belong to someone important.

"Your father is waiting," Owen had said.

"Is that—" she whispered to Roger. "Is that your—I mean—is the *king* in there?"

Roger gave her a look that said, *Of course.*

Mella's hands reached up to pat at her hair, wild and wildblown from her flight on dragonback. Couldn't Roger have said something earlier? Couldn't they have given her two minutes to herself, so she didn't have to face the king—the *king*!—with her hair practically standing on end? There wasn't much she could have done about the dress she'd worn waking and sleeping for days together. Mella even had a fleeting, foolish moment of feeling glad she'd fallen in that murderous pool below the water-fall; at least it had been something like a wash. . . .

Then she was ducking inside the king's tent.

It wasn't really like a tent, she thought. More like a room with walls of red and yellow silk. There was even a carpet underfoot, and a bed in one corner, and chairs gathered around a table, with two men sitting in them. A number of other people were in the room as well, some soldiers, some nobles, and one who was neither. Gwyn was standing so still in a corner that Mella thought most people had probably forgotten he was there. The shepherd had one arm in a linen sling and he met Mella's eyes with a quiet smile and dipped his head to her, as if he were acknowledging a job well done.

One of the men sitting at the table rose; the other started to do so and was waved back into his chair by the first. She knew the sitting man; it was Damien. He looked worn and tired, a white bandage standing out sharply against his black hair; one leg, stretched out before him, was splinted and heavily bandaged.

She knew the standing man, too. He'd grown a

beard since she had seen him pass by the Inn years ago, and his short brown hair was touched with threads of gray. It was so curly it almost hid the simple gold circlet on his head.

Mella glanced around nervously. Should she kneel? But everyone else, including Roger, simply bowed slightly, so Mella just bent her knee and ducked her head.

"So this is the young dragonkeeper?"

Mella changed her mind as the king's voice, not loud but strong, silenced everyone else in the tent. She dropped to her knees and stared fixedly at the king's boots, polished leather laced up over his knees, and bit her lip. Was he angry? At Roger, at her? She'd already faced one angry ruler this day. It didn't seem fair that she should have to deal with a second.

The feet came a little closer, and then a hand came into Mella's view. It touched her chin gently and tipped her head back so that she looked into the king's face.

He's kind, she thought in amazement as he

smiled. There was gentleness in his face, though it was stern about the mouth and worn by worry around the eyes.

"No need for that," the king said, and he took Mella by the hand to lift her to her feet. "So you and my son have been gallivanting all over the wilderness, I hear?"

"Father, we—" Roger broke in.

"Your Majesty—" Wiltain interrupted at the same moment.

The king held up a hand to quiet them both. "Well?" he said to Mella.

And Mella knew just what to answer.

"We had to," she said, looking up into the king's face. "I promised. It was a matter of honor."

The king looked as if he might be about to reply, but Wiltain spoke again. "Your Majesty, I—" This time it was Damien who interrupted.

"Honor?" The king's head turned. So did everyone else's. Damien's dark eyes looked past Mella and glared as though he would set fire to Roger with the force of his gaze alone. "To take sides with our enemy? To aid a *dragon*? To forget the vows you swore? This is *honor*?"

Yes, Damien was definitely angry.

Roger seemed to shrivel by Mella's side. She looked over at him in alarm. He'd spoken up so bravely to the dragon queen, and now he wilted before a mere knight? She drew in a breath to defend Roger, hardly knowing what she was going to say, but the king got there first.

"I believe the prince took an oath to keep the kingdom safe from dragons," he said. "He appears to have done that most effectively—he and his friend."

Roger looked startled.

"Your Majesty," Wiltain insisted. He was the kind of person who would always get heard, Mella realized, just because he wouldn't stop talking until it happened.

"Yes, Wiltain?" the king said patiently.

"We could send out word to stop the army's retreat! Sire, we must defend the kingdom. We cannot simply *leave* now that we know what these—

these beasts—are capable of!" He flapped a hand vaguely at Damien.

A shout of protest leaped up in Mella's throat. This couldn't happen. Not after Roger had promised. Not after the dragons had trusted them. *Humans have no honor,* Kieron had said. Were they going to prove him right?

"Father," Roger insisted, his voice shrill with alarm. "Father!"

But the king's look silenced Wiltain, stopped Roger, and made Mella swallow her objections.

"I believe my son negotiated a treaty," the king said, his eyes nearly as fierce as Damien's. "Are you suggesting that we break it?"

Wiltain's face turned nearly as red as his wine-colored coat.

"I—that is—no, of course not, Your Majesty. I merely—"

"I'm relieved to hear it," King Astor said sharply. "Since the other side of the bargain has been kept, we must do our part. Captain!" Owen looked up. "We will join the retreat. We wish to demonstrate goodwill, so as promptly as possible, please."

Mella could hardly believe how efficiently the king's orders were carried out. The tent disappeared from around them, the carpets were rolled up practically under their feet, carts were filled, and horses were saddled with startling speed. Wiltain was fussing over the girth on his horse, and the king was settling an argument over whether Damien would ride or be carried in a litter, and Roger and Mella stood still in the center of the storm of activity.

"Here." Mella remembered the queen's gift to her and pulled one of the dragontooth necklaces over her head. "This is yours. From the queen. She said—she said it would mark you as a dragonfriend. Forever."

Roger stared at the pendant in his hand as if he were hypnotized by its sway. "But it's—but that's—"

A shadow fell over the necklace, and Mella looked up to see Gwyn standing against the light.

Slowly, without asking, he leaned over to gather up the swinging piece of ivory in one hand. The movement loosened something around his own neck, and it swung forward into the light—a much older piece of ivory, worn thin and yellow, its once-sharp point blunted by time.

But Roger was looking past the shepherd, toward Damien, as, under the king's stern gaze, he climbed reluctantly into a litter slung between two horses. And Mella remembered that the Defender had worn something similar around his neck, a long, thin tooth on a fine gold chain. And *he* was certainly no dragonfriend.

Gwyn's eyes lifted up to the mountain towering over them. "Saw them, did you?" he asked, his voice low. "*Talked* to them? Like my father said— the true dragons?"

Mella nodded, and a slow smile spread across the shepherd's face.

The king was on horseback now, and a shout came from Owen. "Mount up! All mounted to ride!"

Dragons were full of mysteries, Mella decided. And so were rulers and knights and even shepherds, and her brain was worn out trying to decipher it all. Right now she simply wanted to be back home, caring for her herd, enduring the scolding she was sure she'd get for worrying her parents, safe away from kings and queens and puzzles and quests and things an innkeeper's daughter was probably not meant to understand.

A soldier at Gwyn's side handed him the reins of a nervous roan mare, who tugged at his arm, pulling him a step or two away from the children. The shepherd swung into the saddle with a glance down at Roger and Mella that might almost have been of envy. As Roger pulled the leather thong over his head and tucked the tooth safely inside his shirt, two more soldiers hurried up, holding the reins of a black mare for Roger and a gentle gray one for Mella.

But Roger hesitated, even as Owen called again, "All mount!" He was looking up at the mountain just as Gwyn had done.

"I wish Alyas had stayed," he murmured. "It wouldn't have been safe, I know. But I wanted to say good-bye."

Looking at the wistful expression on Roger's face, Mella thought of something to make him feel better.

"He's going to write a song about us," she said. "He's a bard. It'll be about the rescue of the Egg. He said, with two such heroes, it should be remembered for a thousand years."

Roger blinked. "Heroes? He said that?"

"Heroes who might learn to be a trifle less impetuous, next time," King Astor said, riding up alongside them. The saddle skirts on his gray stallion were red velvet and golden silk, and they nearly swept the ground. "Bards do tend to exaggerate. Mount up. They're waiting."

One of the soldiers gave Mella a quick boost into the saddle. Roger swung on unaided, while the king took his place at the head of their small party.

Mella eyed Roger's bent head, the slump of his

shoulders. He had only heard the king's reproof, she realized, not the compliment behind it.

"He just called you a hero," she whispered loudly. "You're being stupid again!"

Roger's head came up, and she saw a startled smile cross his face as they followed the king in the path of the retreating army, heading for Dragonsford and home.